Francis Constantine Hill

Robed and Crowned

A Memorial of Mrs. Nettie Hill Weeden

Francis Constantine Hill

Robed and Crowned
A Memorial of Mrs. Nettie Hill Weeden

ISBN/EAN: 9783337267575

Printed in Europe, USA, Canada, Australia, Japan

Cover: Foto ©Raphael Reischuk / pixelio.de

More available books at **www.hansebooks.com**

ROBED AND CROWNED

A MEMORIAL OF

MRS. NETTIE HILL WEEDEN

BY REV. FRANCIS C. HILL

WITH

SELECTIONS FROM HER WRITINGS

AND

SKETCHES AND PAPERS

FROM

Rev. B. M. Adams, D.D.	Rev. I. Simmons, D.D.
Rev. A. C. Bowdish, D.D.	Rev. E. Warriner
Rev. W. T. Pray	Rev. John Parker

Mrs. Frances E. Hill Johnson

AND OTHERS

NEW YORK
PRINTED BY HUNT & EATON
150 Fifth Avenue
1891

TO

THE CHERISHED AND LOVING FRIENDS OF

OUR DEAR DAUGHTER,

WHO HAS CROSSED IN TRIUMPH THE STREAM OF DEATH,

AND

WAVES A WELCOME

AND

BECKONS US ONWARD TO THE OTHER SHORE,

THIS VOLUME

IS

𝔄𝔣𝔣𝔢𝔠𝔱𝔦𝔬𝔫𝔞𝔱𝔢𝔩𝔶 𝔈𝔫𝔰𝔠𝔯𝔦𝔟𝔢𝔡.

"Would you know more of her character? Follow her to heaven and
angels will tell it you."

INTRODUCTION.

VERY soon after the death of our dear daughter a letter was received from a friend, in which he said :

"It is the judgment of many of our preachers who were so well acquainted with your now sainted daughter that more of her life-character and work should be given to the public and her numerous friends than is furnished in the short obituary that appears in *The Christian Advocate.*

"And it is also the opinion of the brethren that you, being best acquainted with her, would be the proper one to write and publish such a memorial."

While the above suggestion found a warm response in our heart, there were reasons that caused us to hesitate. Our love for her while living was deep and intense. Her death and departure caused no abatement of the same. Largely she yet appears to us as the true ideal of a loving, affectionate child, and of complete Christian womanhood.

With such feelings, could we write an impartial account of her life? Might not our warm admiration of her give an undue coloring to the character we wished to portray? It was possible that such might be the case, yet in our judgment the picture, to be real and just, would even admit of stronger and brighter colors than we have been able to employ. Concerning this we must leave the friends and dear reader to decide.

For many years she kept a diary in which she recorded much of life's happenings, as well as her Christian experience and correspondence. But these were mostly lost or destroyed. Only a small portion have come to our hands from which to write this " memorial," but enough to indicate in some degree the trend and quality of her mind and heart.

We are impressed, however, that they largely fail to represent her. There is needed the *actual presence* to give them effect, the sweetness of voice, the expression of countenance that sometimes became strangely supernatural, the magnetism, or, what better expresses our meaning, the Spirit's light and influence resting upon her, and often attending her ministrations. These gave richness and quality to her life and labor, and made her the true evangel she was.

Much of this cannot be written or described by any language we can call to use. In this little volume there is no pretense or claim to special literary merit. It has not been our aim to satisfy a critical taste. Our desire has been to give a simple story of her sweet and beautiful life. Any other attempt would be out of place and would produce an unnatural likeness. To do this we have allowed her, as far as possible, to give her own testimony. This is always spoken or written in the artless simplicity of her nature.

Thus we have followed her through her early years up to womanhood; have watched the dawnings of her religious experience step by step until she becomes a child of the kingdom.

Her *Christian* character was her strength and beauty. This permeated her life and being. Besides this there was little else. Christ had become her true life, and her joy was to declare, "The life I now live in the flesh I live by the faith of the Son of God."

Within that circle she lived and shone with increasing luster, which neither time nor circumstance could dim, growing brighter unto the perfect day.

It is impossible for us to turn our eyes toward the sun and not see its superior light. To look upon a holy life we must see its beauty and feel its elevating power. Such, we trust, may be the results of these pages. Those who desire a closer communion with God, who are longing for a deeper consecration, will here find light and encouragement.

In her experience the way of simple, all-conquering faith will be seen and apprehended. To her heaven and earth were in close proximity. Her hope was strong and steadfast, holding her in the storm and anchoring her to the upper world. But her love was regal. Of all the qualities of her nature this was most prominent, and dominated the rest. It was its constraining force. It shone in her eye, lived in her thoughts, and breathed in her words. It was this that invested her utterances with such marvelous influence; that made her song so potent and angelic.

A heart so loving, so pure, so transparent, must draw from others a loving response. It was even so, as very many were won to Christ by her "work of faith and labor of love." These, begotten to a new life, would first of all love the Author of their salvation, but next would their love turn toward her

who had been so directly instrumental in their conversion; hence the numerous letters received by her
expressing to her their gratitude as the instrument by
which their hearts were won to the Saviour. Upon her
part this love was reciprocal. She had no natural children of her own, but those begotten to Christ by her
were dearly loved. She could appropriate the language of Paul: " But we were gentle among you, even
as a nurse cherisheth her children: . . . We were
willing to have imparted unto you, not the gospel of
God only, but also our own souls, because *ye were
dear unto us.*" Or, like John, to say, " I have no
greater joy than to hear that my children walk in the
truth."

It is interesting to follow her through the dark night
that preceded the dawning of her religious life. We
will be deeply impressed with the thoroughness of the
work. The Spirit's power in her awakening and conviction leaves us no room to doubt its genuineness.
When the change came it was radical; some are
"healed slightly," hers was not of that kind. " Completeness of pardon " was God's method in her intro-
duction into the kingdom. As we follow her until
she comes to the possession of that higher type of

Christian experience and living, we behold the beautiful transformation and are deeply interested. We watch her struggle with the angel until she "seizes the prey," then, "as a bounding hart, flies home" to proclaim out of her heart's experience, "Thy nature and thy name is Love."   .

Few will read this without becoming impressed with a desire to rise to the same plane of enjoyment and spiritual victory. And many who will read of her consecrated labors will put themselves more in union with the Master and become as never before "co-workers together with God."

To the dear friends whose loving contributions appear in this "memorial" we are deeply grateful. These, laid as so many tributes upon the altar of her memory, will go forth to emphasize the divine declaration, "Wisdom is the principal thing," and "the fruit of it is better than gold, yea, than fine gold." And, "they that turn many to righteousness, shall shine as the stars for ever and ever."

We may refer to her contributions of verse scattered through this volume.

She did not claim to be a poetess; yet it was a gift she possessed, though she never sought to cultivate it. Her nature was poetical. With a strong and vivid imagination that hung its pictures around the chambers of her soul, it was only natural she should speak them out in verse and song.

From her childhood she was accustomed to write verses. Sometimes when moving about the house, or going and returning from school, she would be seized with a thought, and often paused to write it down, perhaps making a post or the fence the tablet. It was the outcome and overflow of thoughts that struggled for expression in simple verse. These were a part of herself, and represented the inward workings of her heart.

Some of the pieces recorded in this volume have merit, and they will be read with interest, because they had their birth in her by the Holy Spirit. We call up "Sweetly Resting." It was simply the outspoken "rest" of her own soul. It became very popular as a song of the "higher life," and many were by its influence helped over into the sunny land of perfect love.

Another, found on page —, wonderfully illustrates the language of the evangelical prophet: "For ye shall go out with joy, and be led forth with peace:

the mountains and the hills shall *break forth before you unto singing,* and all the trees of the fields shall clap their hands."

In this song her joy, like Jordan's swelling flood, breaks over its banks. It is Beulah land indeed. Many have caught an inspiration while reading or singing it akin to her own.

Her simple " Birthday " tributes to " loved ones at home " are but the expression of a love deep and intense, a very passion in her soul. To read them will incite in some a stronger love for home and friends, and cause them to prize and enjoy them more before death comes to divide the circle.

We may not omit to notice the last product of her mind and pen, entitled " A Clean Sweep for God." It deserves a place in the heart and theology of every true Christian. It is the very embodiment of the body, soul, and spirit requirement of the Gospel. Aside from its poetical character it is emphasized by her surroundings when written. Literally with feet in the river of death, with soul aspiring, with will and purpose unfettered, with every thought brought into captivity, it found for its utterance, " A Clean Sweep for God." It was her " swan song," and as such will be read and prized by her many loving friends.

ROBED AND CROWNED, the title selected for this "memorial," is not merely sentimental. It comes to our mind as a fitting and legitimate one. In the arch of her life she builded; this is the key-stone. That mysterious heaven-sent "vision" herein recorded produced a transforming power in her life. It became the inspiration and girding of her soul to holier experiences and enlarged activities.

For more than a year there has been upon the heart of the writer of these pages a sacred responsibility. We have prayed that the record we shall make of a life so loving and useful may by the Holy Spirit go forth to bless other hearts, and continue to be a ministry of good in the years to come. Upon our part the writing of this memorial has been a tribute of affection; a sadly pleasing task, often bedewing the page with tears; with heart sorely chastened because here "we shall see her face no more," not yet understanding why so much of love should thus early be removed from our home; yet the cup placed in our hands we will drink, looking for strength and grace to write "Jesus" on the broken crystals of our hopes; on

the white casket covered with flowers; on the grave;
on the vacant chair; pressing our sorrowful heart
closer to his bosom.

> " For we know, when our silver chord is loosed
>   And the veil is rent away,
> Not long and dark shall the passage be
>   To the realms of endless day.
> For the eye that shuts in the mortal hour
>   Shall open the next in bliss ;
> *Her welcome* shall sound in the heavenly world,
>   Ere the farewell is hushed in this."

CONTENTS.

2

CHAPTER XIX.

CHAPTER XX.

CHAPTER XXI.

CHAPTER XXII.

CHAPTER XXIII.

CHAPTER XXIV.

CONTENTS. 19

ILLUSTRATIONS.

ROBED AND CROWNED.

CHAPTER I.

NETTIE HILL WEEDEN, whose sweet and pure life became a blessing to so many, whose experience we may well recount and hold up as an example, was born in the village of Hempstead, Long Island, State of New York, February 15, 1844. She was the eldest child of Rev. Francis C. and Sarah Hill.

Of her ancestors, those upon her maternal side were from Long Island, mostly residing in the town of Hempstead—old families, whose history reaches back to the early settlement of the town.

Her paternal grandfather was born in Harwington, Conn. Her grandmother, Sally Lockwood, was born in Norwalk, Fairfield County, Conn. Her lineage may be traced to the early settlement of that ancient town. Her great-grandmother was from Massachusetts, and lived in the village of Deerfield when it was attacked by the Indians and a terrible massacre took place in the year 1704, concerning which the historian writes: " What a scene is that upon which the sun rises on that morning! Forty or more mangled corpses, the snow crimsoned with blood, the homes of the murdered inhabitants on fire ! One hundred and eight men, women, and children driven out through the snow, some of them barefooted and thinly clad, to take up their march toward Canada; some to perish in the wilderness, some to starve, others to fall by the tomahawk by the way, while others, who survived the sufferings and hardships of that terrible march, reached Canada feeble and exhausted, more dead than alive." This great-grandparent was one of the number, and was at that time a little girl of eight years of age. She, after suffering incredible hardships, was redeemed and returned again to the ruined home in Deerfield.

In the year 1819 Nettie's grandparents removed from Norwalk, in Fairfield County, across the Sound to Huntington.

There were born to them in that place five children —four sons and one daughter. Francis C., the father of Nettie, was the third, and spent the early years of his life in that place.

Her mother, Sarah Baker, was born in the city of New York, but removed at an early age to Hempstead.

We do not wish to dwell longer upon her ancestry,

yet we cannot refrain from making a more extended mention of this last named grandmother.

Upon removing to Long Island she and her husband united themselves with the people called Methodists, at that time feeble in influence and few in numbers. The Presbyterian church dated its history with the first settlement of the town. It had a large membership and was the controlling church.

Here, as in many other places on the island, the Methodists were not regarded with favor. They were looked upon as a " fanatical set," and were every-where "spoken against;" yet the irrepressible Methodist preacher insisted upon the privilege of preaching in the towns and villages of the island.

They had but few churches of their own. School-houses were frequently closed against them, hence the word was preached by them in private houses, and often in barns.

One of the places opened and to which these circuit-riders were invited was in that grandparent's home. Here they were always welcome. If they desired rest for a day or two after traveling their long circuit, they found it. If their garments needed repair, here were found hands that willingly performed for them the required service.

That grandmother was a devout Christian, and a "helper" of those who preached the Gospel. She was a woman of deep and positive convictions, and carried them out in her life and experience. She has been dead more than thirty years, yet our reminiscences of her are as vivid as if she had passed but yesterday. She had no written memorial in this world, but her rich faith and holy works built for her a monument that still survives. In our memory she still lives as a saint. Time was not needed to canonize her in human hearts; that was done before she went to her reward.

From our hearts to-day we echo the words,

> " Happy he
> With such a mother; faith in womankind
> Beats with his blood, and trust in all things high
> Comes easy to him."

The promise, " And it shall come to pass in the last days, saith God, I will pour out of my Spirit upon all flesh : and your sons and your daughters shall prophesy," found a fulfillment in her life. Gifted in speech and song, she was ever ready to bear a part in the meetings and services of those early times.

By courage and wonderful perseverance she gathered together the children of the neighborhood and organized the first Sabbath-school in the town; and because no better place could be found, held it in her husband's work-shop.

For eleven years she superintended that school, soon removing it to a place large enough to accom-

modate its growing numbers. Several distinct revivals broke out during those years in the school,
and many of the converts came into the church,
lived pious lives, and died happy and triumphant
deaths. Among the number may be specially mentioned Nettie's uncle, Dr. Asa Hill, whose excellent
life closed in Norwalk, Conn., in November, 1873.

Family traits and characteristics are sometimes
handed down to posterity.

With this excellent woman such was the case. Four
of her sons became preachers of the Gospel; others of
the children were prominent members of the Church.
But especially did her mantle of faith fall upon
her grandchild. Many that remembered the loving
zeal and work of the grandparent, when they saw
and heard Nettie, would exclaim, "How much like
her sainted grandmother!" And there was, indeed,
a striking resemblance between the two; both baptized with the Spirit of the Master, each burning with
a holy desire for the salvation of others, possessing
gifts of a similar character, with a faith that relied upon God, and a persuasive eloquence that brought precious fruitage. So the godly grandmother lived again
in the granddaughter. And she, being long since dead,
spoke again from the lips of our now sainted Nettie,
while together they now shine with the celestial brightness of stars, having turned many to righteousness.

CHAPTER II.

Childhood Days.—Baptism.—In a Preacher's Home.—Habit of Attending House of God.—Early Impressed with Religious Truth.—Prayer a Habit.—Joyful Childhood.—Photographs of Childhood.

WE return now to her childhood days. These did not differ in most respects from the generality of children. As a child she was not unusually attractive. Strangers would see nothing in her beyond the ordinary character of childhood, never suspecting the mine of hidden wealth that slumbered beneath that unassuming exterior; but time and education, together with the work of grace, did develop and bring forth those resources that made her life so pure and useful. By her friends she was much esteemed and loved. Her parents sought to bring her up in the "nurture and admonition of the Lord." Her maternal grandmother, who for many years was a member of the family, took a deep interest in this her only grandchild. She, like "Lois," young Timothy's grandmother, possessed the faith that was to be transmitted by mild and loving instructions—by a sweet example—to the child also.

When but four months old she was taken to the

church in Hempstead, and at the altar where her father and mother first gave their hearts to God, and where they together stood when united in the holy bands of marriage, there this their first-born was consecrated to God in Christian baptism, the service being performed by the Rev. W. K. Stopford of precious memory.

From that hour she became a covenant child, and through all her subsequent life she shared the blessings of her covenant-keeping God.

In May, 1844, when but three months old, her father was received into the New York Conference. His first appointment was at Cornwall Bridge and Cornwall, in Connecticut. It was here, surrounded by the mountains and pure atmosphere of that State, she began her itinerant life, a loved one, in the home of a Methodist preacher. This continued with but little intermission until her death. In her infancy she was taken to the house of God, like young Samuel; she almost dwelt in the sanctuary.

This habit so early formed became a part of her maturer life, and only ceased with her death. Her life-experience may well be declared in the language of another, "Lord, I have loved the courts of thy house." So uniform and constant was her attendance during all her early life that most people thought her to be a Christian.

" And ye shall teach them to your children, speaking of them, when thou liest down, and when thou risest up." This charge, given by Moses to the children of Israel, was felt by her parents to be the secret of a good and useful life; hence they sought to act accordingly.

Much care and pains were taken to impress her with the importance of early piety—to know and love Jesus in her childhood. And very often she was taken alone in retirement to kneel beside her father or mother in prayer, where for her the blessings of God were invoked.

In recounting her experience she often referred to those early religious teachings, and delighted to speak of them as the direct means through which she gave herself to God. She did not remember the time when she commenced to pray. It began in her very early childhood, and it is doubtful if ever a day passed that she did not kneel in prayer. It was as much a habit with her as to eat or sleep.

In her childhood there was a sweetness of disposition that brought love in return. She was a happy, joyful child, knowing no care or trouble. She often declared, when alluding to her early life: " Mine was a happy childhood. I knew no care or anxiety, every want of my life was met by my dear father and mother and blessed grandmother; indeed, I did not think any thing could injure me so long as they were near."

There are now in the family several photographs, taken at different times during her childhood. Some of these we produce in this volume. They reveal an expression of innocence and love, so much like her character. They continued to unfold until she became the holy, godly woman of her maturer life.

CHAPTER III.

CONFERENCE APPOINTMENT.—SECOND YEAR.—FATAL EPIDEMIC.—AUTO-
BIOGRAPHY OF A. GRIFFING.—SORROWFUL DAYS.—STEAM-BOAT EXCUR-
SION.—DEATH IN THE PARSONAGE.—NETTIE'S FIRST SORROW.—VERSES.

WHEN Nettie was four years of age, by Conference appointment her parents removed to
Orient, a beautiful little village situated on the east
end of the north branch of Long Island. The second
year of their residence there, being the year 1849, the
community was visited by a fatal epidemic. It will
be remembered that that was the year when the scourge
of cholera fell upon our country with desolating effect.
In this quiet village, almost surrounded by the sea, and
so far distant from any populous city, it was thought
the plague might not come. But in this we were
doomed to disappointment. It came in the form of
dysentery, having many of the features of the cholera.
The physicians called it the "cholera dysentery." As
what followed was a part of our dear Nettie's experience, we here insert an account published at that
time in the autobiography of Augustus Griffing, an
aged and honorable citizen living in Orient. Mr.
Griffing says: "During the autumn of 1849 our beau-

tiful village was visited by a mortal sickness. Rev.
Francis C. Hill was at that time a resident, with an
interesting family of a wife and two daughters of four
and six years of age. The youngest, Anna Landon,
fell a victim to the dire calamity. For some time
previous an extensive drought had been experienced.
For a number of weeks we had no cooling showers,
no thunder or lightning. The earth became excess-
ively dry and parched.

"About the middle of August a number of cases
occurred, but so mild as not to give alarm. It commenced among the children; but such was its progress
(for it was not confined to the young) it seized upon
the middle-aged and the old alike. Within two weeks
not less than sixty cases were reported within a distance of little over a half-mile. In the street leading
from the main road to the wharf scarcely a house or
family escaped. In some homes one half were prostrated. In others four out of five were seized. There
were not enough of persons well to care for the sick.
Sometimes two of the dead were interred at the same
time. Within one hundred yards of the Methodist
parsonage there were twelve deaths.

"There was scarcely a house in the whole street
but one or more of its inmates were removed by
death. It seemed as if our beautiful village had
become transformed into a Golgotha. An incident

occurred at this time which may illustrate the condition of things. An excursion party on board the steamer *Statesman*, from Sag Harbor, touched at our wharf. A large company of men, women, and children landed and commenced to stroll up through the village. Not meeting with scarce an individual, for the place had the stillness of the Sabbath, after proceeding some distance they met a person who informed them of the mortality at that time prevailing. They were panic-stricken, and hastened to the boat with terror and alarm being depicted on every countenance. At that time many in the street were sick and numbers dying. In one house two bodies lay dead and unburied."

Such was Mr. Griffing's account of the fearful mortality that there prevailed.

It was, indeed, a dark and sorrowful time in our parsonage home. Four were down at once with the malady—father, mother, Nettie, and Anna; all prostrated by the disease.

Our youngest, Anna Landon, a sweet child of four summers, was taken from us, we sharing the desolating woe that swept through the village.*

---

* Two years later there occurred in that same parsonage another sad and sorrowful event. The young and beautiful wife of Dr. L. S. Weed passed away from the clouds and sorrow of earth to the sunshine and joy of heaven.

The loss of little Anna was Nettie's first great sorrow. Their lives had run together in a single groove, inseparable. They ate, slept, and played together. Her grief was great and she seemed inconsolable. She never lost sight of it. Her little angel sister seemed ever to be present with her. Those who have been familiar with her ministrations will call to mind her touching allusions to the companion of her childhood. Through all the years, as often as she could, she visited the cemetery where she was buried, when she would bedew that little grave with affection's tears, and, kneeling upon the same, would commune with her Saviour and the spirit of the departed loved one, and there renewedly consecrate herself to a holier life and more earnest and devoted labor.

After the death of that sister her uncle, Dr. Asa Hill, sent her the following simple verses, which she learned and ever after loved to repeat:

> I had a little sister dear,
>   Not many days ago ;
> And when I think of her
>   The tear unbidden seems to flow.

> She was the youngest of our flock,
>   And scarcely four years old ;
> It was a painful thing to lose
>   The pet lamb of the fold.

3

Her gentle spirit, light and free,
　Was gladsome as the morn ;
And, O, it was a joy to me
　That such a child was born.

I see her little toys about,
　And sigh, but sigh in vain ;
I ne'er shall hear the joyous shout
　Of sister dear again.

I speak her name, no answering voice
　Breaks through the silent air ;
I turn at every little noise,
　But Anna is not there.

A heavy thought is on my heart,
　A load of grief and pain ;
That we so soon should have to part,
　Nor meet on earth again.

She was a little angel, sent
　To cheer us on our way ;
And He who kindly gave her
　Took my sister dear away.

Now when I lift my voice in prayer,
　At morn, at noon, at even,
The eye of faith beholds her there,
　At God's right hand, in heaven.

Who can doubt but that she did really experience
the fellowship of that twin spirit during all the subsequent years of her life? In it there was something
more than imagination. "For *ye are come* to the spirits
of just men made perfect"—not will come in the future,

but are now already introduced to their presence. We
have a letter written to her husband on her thirty-fifth
birthday. In it she alludes to her happy, joyous childhood; she speaks of memories of home, of father,
mother, and dear grandmother. "Then I recall the
merry laugh of my little angel sister, Anna, with gentle
form and golden curls. O, she was a precious link in
the chain that connects those scenes with to-day. I
feel stronger and life is purer because of the rays of
light that have gleamed down the years upon me from
that angel one. Taken from my side so soon!—a bud
too fair for earthly blooming, transplanted early to a
celestial clime. I think she will be the first to sing a
'welcome home to me.'"

In Nettie's last sickness among the blessed realities
anticipated by her was the meeting with her Saviour
and *sister*, after so long a separation.

"Ma, do you think Anna will know me?" and with
the question a smile played across her almost seraphic
face. In her heart there was no doubt of instant and
full recognition. That feeling was shared by other
members of the family.

Among her letters we find one written by myself,
bearing date September, 1890. From that letter we
extract the following, which seems prophetic: "To-
morrow, the 19th day of September, will mark forty
years since our dear little Anna Landon passed away

from this world of strife and sorrow. At half-past
ten in the evening her life went out, or was exchanged
for the ever-enduring one. O, it was a dark, sad night
in that parsonage! Heaven only knew the heart-aching
of that hour.

"Forty years! It appears a long time to us. To
her gentle spirit it doubtless seems as yesterday. All
these years she has represented our home where there
are no tears. Such is not the case here, for even now
is our heart sorrowful and our eyes filled with tears.
Memory opens the mystic doors of the past and we
see it all again."

But faith can sing:

"We have a child, a sweet girl, her age we cannot tell,
For they reckon not by years or months where she has gone to
    dwell.
To us for nearly four anxious years her joyous smiles were
    given,
And then she bade farewell to earth and went to live in heaven.

"We cannot tell what form is hers—what looks she weareth now,
Nor guess how bright a glory crowns her shining seraph brow.
The thoughts that fill her sinless soul, the bliss which she doth
    feel,
Are numbered with the secret things which God will not reveal.

"We know we shall meet our child (her mother dear and I)
When God for aye shall wipe away all tears from every eye.
Whatever befalls her brother or sisters twain her bliss shall never
    cease;
Their lot may here be grief and fear, but hers is certain peace.

"When we think of what our darling is and what we still
  must be;
When we muse on that world's perfect bliss and this world's
  misery ;
When we groan beneath this load of care and feel this grief
  and pain,
O, we had rather lose our other three than have her here again."

In a little more than two weeks from the date of
this letter Nettie went to join little Anna, and another representative from our earthly home was in
that heavenly land.

CHAPTER IV.

Her School Life.—Frequent Removals Unfriendly to Study.—
Music.—Mother's Drill.—First Organ.—Competent Teacher
Obtained.—Its Power for Good.

THUS far we have sketched Nettie's birth, her ancestry, and something of her early experience of joys and sorrows.

We come now to speak of her school life and education. This commenced when quite young, and continued almost without intermission until she was eighteen years of age. The Methodist itinerant life—where frequent removals occurred—did not afford the best opportunities for instruction. The ordinary country schools were not usually of a high grade. Putting these things together, the difficulty of acquiring an education will be largely understood and felt.

These were among the embarrassments of her school life. In later days none regretted them more than she. Still her acquirements were equal to, if not above, the average, and very creditable to herself. When about twelve years of age she attended a female seminary in the village where her parents resided, during which time she made rapid advancement in her studies.

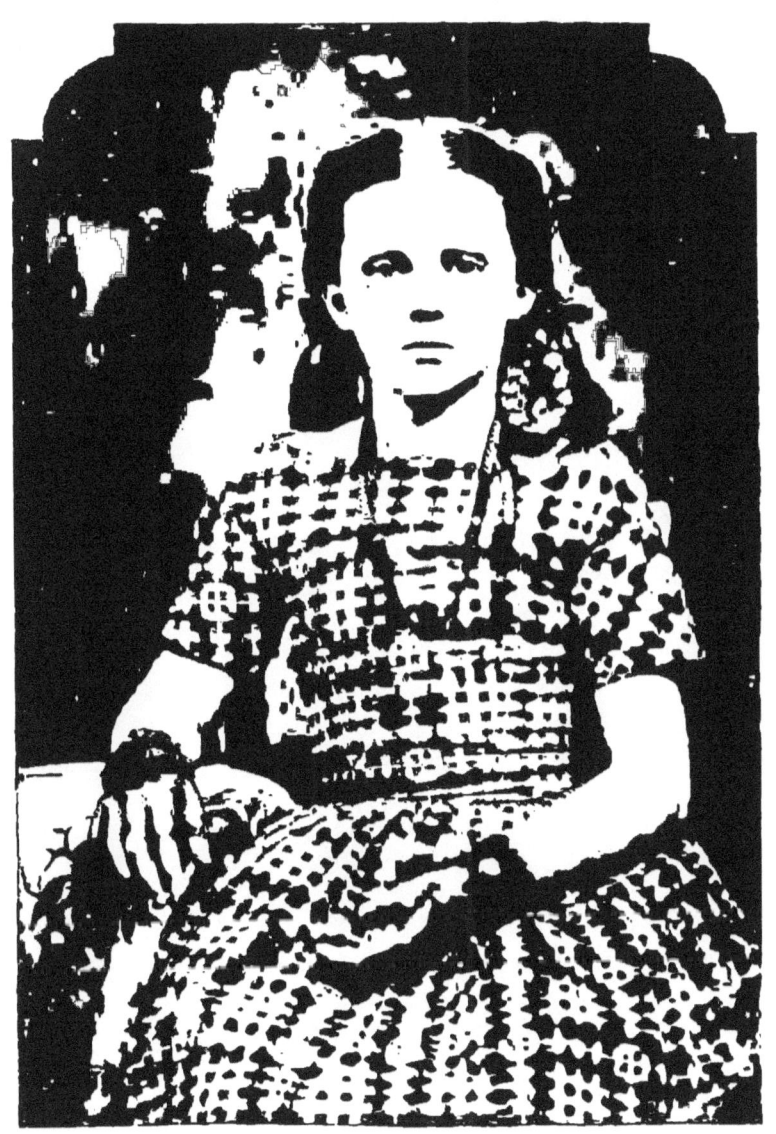

NETTIE AT ELEVEN YEARS OF AGE.

Two years later she attended the Franklinville Academy. At that time Professor Joseph Hallock, now editor and publisher of the *Christian at Work*, was the principal. Here she acquired a better discipline of study, and her mind and intellect seemed to find a larger development. In most of her studies she was successful. She learned as never before the use of words; she was a good grammarian, and when she came to speak in public she was not only ready of utterance, but her language was chaste and correct. But often she expressed regrets that she could not have attended the advanced schools and seminaries that are now so numerous, to have prepared herself more fully for the public labors she felt called to perform.

Added to her school life, as we have briefly endeavored to state it, we desire not to omit her musical education.

During much of her girlhood this was largely omitted. It was because in the country towns where she resided the opportunities for the study of music, either vocal or instrumental, were very largely wanting, and teachers were both poor and scarce. Moreover, such was the small and meager salary of her father that the purchase of a piano or organ seemed to be out of the question. She had a longing desire to become acquainted with music, and her parents were very anxious to give her the opportunity.

During these passing years, with all the disadvantages we have mentioned, she had one faithful and loving instructor in singing Her mother, one of the sweet singers, with a voice of great richness and melody, gave her lessons.

She would sit by her for hours and teach her the art of song—the importance of distinctly speaking the words set to the music, a part too much neglected.

This faithful drill, from so good and faithful a teacher, was of the utmost value to her. When she herself became a teacher of vocal as well as instrumental music its results were seen. And when she began to "sing for Jesus" she could truthfully say, "I will sing with the spirit, and with the understanding also." And from these early instructions given her she was able to give what Paul calls "a distinction of sounds," and to "utter by the tongue words easy to be understood," so that the people should "know what was spoken," and when they heard the song and understood the words would say, "Amen."

The day came at last when, by much economizing and sacrifice in the preacher's family, a small organ was purchased.

It was a great event when that little instrument

was introduced into the parsonage. Nettie was delighted, and father and mother shared the joy.

Soon a teacher was found, and her drill in music commenced. Some time after her father was stationed in the city of Brooklyn, where for nine years she had the advantages of the best and most competent teachers that could be obtained.

This department of her education was of great value to her. For years she was herself a teacher, giving instructions on piano and organ and in vocal music, and by her skill and aptitude was able to bring forward her pupils rapidly to good acquirements.

It became a source of pecuniary advantage to her; but, more than all, it gave her a power to edify and bless the people. A great factor for good was her power of song, accompanied with music either on piano or organ.

CHAPTER V.

Life Pleasant.—Serious Illness.—Constitution Injured.—First Experience Away from Home at School.—Her Attachment to Home.—A Birth in the Parsonage.

AS a beautiful summer morning dawns on the world, with soft breezes and a cloudless sky, so it was with Nettie's early life. Except the serious illness and loss of her little sister when at Orient her life was much like a June morning. Without care or anxiety, she was a joyous, happy child.

But there are few days in the year when from morn to even there are no passing clouds. So with her life. There must come shadows as well as sunshine, and she began to experience what in later life she would sometimes repeat :

" Life is real, life is earnest."

When fourteen years of age she was stricken with fever, which brought her down near the gates of death. This illness was protracted for several weeks. Upon her recovery it was found the effects of the disease and the medical treatment had impaired that beautiful, and what seemed to be a perfect, constitution. The physician under whose treatment she was placed was of the "old school order." He believed in calomel first, last, and all the time. With this mineral poison she was liberally supplied until salivated and constitutionally broken. From these effects she never recovered. They laid the foundation of ills that followed her and eventually destroyed her life. She appeared to be strong and healthy, but it is doubtful if a week of her life passed without suffering some form of pain, constantly reminding her that indeed the "seeds of death were sown in her mortal body." This was a part of the cross she was to bear; but the discipline of suffering was patiently borne, and its ministry was to bring her nearer to the heart of her Saviour.

When sixteen years of age she went from Whitestone, where she resided, to Huntington to attend school. This was her first experience away from home, and to her it was a trying ordeal—absent from father and mother, among strangers. Letters written by her at that time show how her very life was bound up in her home. Upon her return never was there a glader heart than hers.

Her home was to her, if possible, a conception of heaven; and this feeling never abated. It remained after her marriage, when she had a home of her own. Her intense love for her parents almost amounted to

idolatry.   In later life, when absent, her letters written from time to time breathed the same affection and
longing for home, and often found expression in the
following words :

> "And if I e'er in heaven appear,
>   A father's holy prayer,
> A mother's hand and gentle tear,
> That pointed to a Saviour dear,
>   Have led the wanderer there."

During the year 1860, while residing at Whitestone,
there occurred an event of great interest to the family, and to Nettie in particular.   It was the birth of a
little sister.

Eleven years had passed since the death of little
Anna Landon. Nettie had become partially recon-
ciled to her loss, though the heart-wound was yet un-
healed.

During all these years, so far as childhood companionship was concerned, she was alone. Now this
new advent filled her heart with joy. Her cup
seemed full to overflowing. All the fullness of her
loving heart went to meet the little one, which
she not only took to her arms, but to her heart
also.

She assumed much of the care of her baby sister,
and became to her a second mother. This was not
a momentary passion, to weary in caring for the little

stranger, but it remained and became intensified as long as she lived. Only one other occasion occurred that brought out in her such sisterly affection. It was seven years later, when there came another addition to that home in the form of a little boy, of which we shall speak later on.

CHAPTER VI.

Removal to Glen Cove.—From Childhood Into Womanhood.—Early Habits.—Grandmother's Care.—Her Death.—Singular Watch-night Services.

CONFERENCE year had closed and a removal takes place. Glen Cove follows Whitestone. This for the two following years is to be Nettie's home. Her life was gliding on, unmarked by any remarkable or important events. She was now passing from a child to womanhood. Her mind was maturing with her physical powers. By friends old and young in the church and neighborhood she was esteemed and loved. Her life and deportment were in keeping with the strictest propriety.

Her habit of church-going was as uniform and regular as if she were one of its best members. During the first year of her residence in Glen Cove she sustained a great loss in the death of Mrs. Phebe Baker, her maternal grandmother, who for a number of years had been a member of our home, mostly from the time of Nettie's birth. For this grandmother Nettie always felt a deep affection, and the grandmother most tenderly loved this her only grandchild.

She had given much care in her training and instruction. She was a sincere Christian, and by her
life and precept contributed not a little in bringing
Nettie forward in the path of virtue. In that grandparent she saw the life of a true Christian illustrated. She sadly felt her departure, and ever after
would speak of her dear grandmother with affection,
and as one of the cherished ones she expected to meet
in her bright home beyond. Years after, on her
thirty-first birthday, when writing a birthday greeting
to her husband, she recalls some of the important
events of her life, and says : " Then a few years farther on and the darked-winged angel threw a shadow
again over our happy home. One whose feet, weary
with life's journey, whose heart had so often been
saddened, from whose gentle face the roses of life
seemed to wither and fade—this dear one now stood
upon ' Jordan's banks,' ready to go when she heard
out of the tempest the message ; and she passed over
in triumph. Good-bye, my darling grandmother!
Your example has taught me to bear hardness as a
good soldier. Your feet now stand upon the immortal shore. Farewell ; we'll meet again."

During her residence here there occurred a little
event which, while it may not prove her to have been
a Christian, will disclose some of her heart exercises, and point as an index-finger to the coming hour,

not far distant, when she would be enrolled among the dear children of God.

During the winter of 1862 a watch-night service had been appointed by her father. The evening came, a most bitterly cold night. The wind blew with the violence of a gale, and a deep snow lay upon the ground. The hour arrived, the church was opened and lighted. Not more than a half-dozen persons came. Nettie and her father were there. The pastor became discouraged at the small number present, and announced that there would be no service, and made preparation to return home.

Nettie addressed her father thus : " Pa, I desire to remain here with Nellie and Susie " (two young ladies, sisters of Rev. J. V. Saunders) "and spend the evening as you have done, by watching the old year out and the new one in."

The father could not certainly object. They assured the sexton that the lights would be put out and the doors locked. Thus they were allowed to remain. But how would they occupy those two hours and a half in that lonely church on till the midnight watch? Neither of the three were at that time Christians, though much alike in their outward attendance upon religious services. An account of that watch-night has been furnished by one of the three. She said :

" Nettie laid out the plan. We began by singing

a few hymns; then one of our number read a chapter from the Bible; then we sang again; then we conversed a little in an undertone. As the solemn hour of midnight drew nigh a deep solemnity seemed to come over us. We had been thinking and speaking about the expiring year—how many had died, and how good the Lord had been to us. And then what of the future? With such thoughts pressing upon us we knelt in silence when the solemn, mystic hour was reached and passed. We arose from our knees to break the silence by wishing each other a 'happy new year,' while Nettie's face was bathed in tears."

None but God knows what promises of amended life were there made, what solemn vows were registered in heaven. Those three young persons, not professing Christians, were led at the midnight hour of the expiring year to *watch* and *wait*—for what? Whatever it was, God gave it to them. Yet how many members of the church were either at home asleep or enjoying themselves in social pleasure while these girls waited to watch out the expiring year kneeling at God's altar in the sanctuary.

4

CHAPTER VII.

TWO years were yet the limit of the pastoral term,
and how quickly they passed. Nettie's next home
was in Carlton Avenue in the goodly city of Brooklyn. When the patriarch Jacob was returning to his
father's house after a sojourn of twenty-one years in
Syria he came to "Mahanaim," when it was said,
"There the angels of God met him." The influence
of this rare manifestation was with him to the end of
his earthly journey.

For nineteen years Nettie had itinerated with her
parents, forming many pleasant associations. In all
of these places she had gone out and in with the
Lord's people as if she had been a child of God. But
as yet no clear, distinct Christian life had been reached.
At the best she was nothing more than a "proselyte
of the gate."

This, her new home, is made sacred and hallowed
as the place where God came to her, and where she
received the "white stone" and the "new name."

In the warm and cordial greetings received by the preacher and his family Nettie came in for a goodly share. If there were pleasant things (and there were many), she, our dear child, shared them in common with us. She at once entered the Sunday-school and became a member of one of the adult Bible-classes, having for her teacher Brother W. H. Wilson, a man standing high in the estimation of the church and school. To him, as her teacher and instructor, she ever felt a debt of gratitude.

It was in the Sabbath-school that the great revival of 1864 commenced, embracing in its blessed results the young, the middle-aged, and some advanced in life, until more than three hundred converts were numbered.

For three months nightly the church was thronged. It continued until the session of the Conference. It appeared as if the cloud of God's presence that hovered over that sacred place had, indeed, come to stay. People came from different parts of the city, and even from the country, and knelt at the altar and were saved. This revival was characterized by many wonderful things. Two may be specially mentioned. First, an awful sense of God's presence rested down upon the converted and unconverted; convictions for sin were deep and pungent. Mourners at the altar would cry out in despairing tones, and the voice of weeping could be heard all over the church. Second, the conversions were strong and clear; no comfort or peace came to the penitent until it was spoken by God himself.

This would be known by the shouts of newly born souls. We have more fully referred to this revival because it was here that our dear Nettie was brought to the bosom of her loving Saviour. One Sabbath we were absent by an exchange with a brother in New York. It was during that Sabbath she was under deepest conviction. "Mother," she said, "I must have salvation. I am very unhappy." The mother's reply was, "You can have it; it is for all." She then said, "O, that I could tell father." Mother said, "Get it, Nettie, and then say, 'father, I have it.'" Her tearful answer was, "I will try." That Sunday evening she was one of the first who knelt at the altar when the invitation was given. She returned home feeling no relief. Her awakening was deep; her conviction for sin was intense. For three days the pastor's home was a protracted meeting.

As little of household duties as possible were performed. Our dear one was passing through the throes of spiritual birth, and nothing by day and night was so much in order as prayer and songs of hope and words of encouragement.

Those three days, when darkness was upon her

heart and vision, were like those of Saul of Tarsus before the hands of Ananias were laid upon his eyes. But we will let her describe that wonderful experience—one she often referred to in her religious life. To her friends it seemed strange that she, whose life had been so moral, whose whole deportment so correct, should come to see herself so great a sinner ; for, like the young man who came to Christ, who said, in reference to the commandments, " All these have I kept from my youth up ; what lack I yet ?" why should she come to see herself so great a sinner, and pass through such spiritual agony into the kingdom ?

She herself tells the reason : " *I had neglected Christ !* " That was the secret. " So when the commandment came sin revived, and she died." " The law, taking occasion of the commandment, slew her." Then how sweetly came the loving voice of her Saviour. But we will let her speak for herself :

"Conviction for sin and repentance for the same are described in the word as going before or preceding pardon. I write this because it was a bitter cup that I drank. The sin of my past life, like a deadly serpent, seemed to uncoil itself in my heart. I discovered what I had been ignorant of, that there was a terrible enemy within. Upon my mind there was forced with distinctness the fact that I was under the divine displeasure. It caused me to tremble and

well-nigh despair.   At night I dared not close my eyes
in sleep, lest death might come and I awake with the
lost !   It was not a conviction of outbreaking sin that
so alarmed me.   My life had ranged up to a fair
standard of morality.   Even many of my friends supposed me to be a Christian.   My great sin—that which
towered above all the rest—was *my neglect of Christ.*
And for this it seemed no punishment was too great
for me.   The thunders of a broken law echoed through
all the chambers of my soul, and awakened and
aroused my slumbering conscience, and God did hide
himself from me; and, like the psalmist, 'I found
trouble and sorrow,' and it seemed like a mountain
load, greater than I could bear.   The thought was
presented to my mind, I have crucified the Son of God,
my Saviour, by my long neglect of him, while he only
has been commending himself in love and gentleness
to me.   This seemed a sorrow so deep, so keen, that
it was greater than I could bear.

> " 'I saw One hanging on a tree
>   In agonies of blood;
> He fixed his languid eyes on me,
>   As near his cross I stood.
>
> " 'Sure never till my latest breath
>   Shall I forget that look;
> He seemed to charge me with his death,
>   Though not a word he spoke.'

CARLTON AVENUE CHURCH.

"O, what could I do? In this deep distress, when on the verge of despair, I cried, 'Jesus, save me!' when, quick as the lightning that flashes across the sky, the answer came, 'FORGIVEN!' I am unable to tell the joy of that hour. The very arms of my Saviour seemed to encircle me, while his sweet voice rang through all my being: 'Daughter, thy sins are all forgiven thee.' My heart was full, and in a heavenly ecstacy I sang, for the first time in my life, out of my joyous heart,

> "'I love Jesus, hallelujah!
> Jesus smiles and loves me, too.'

I retired from the altar of the old Carlton Avenue church, where for so many hours I had wept and prayed, a happy, new-born child.

"As I returned home I looked up and saw the moon shining brightly in the heavens. That orb seemed to catch up the glad song and shouted back my pardon. The stars seemed to join the glad anthem and sing together for joy; and angels I knew tuned anew their harps, because the dead was alive, the lost was found. I understood now the apostle's words, 'Old things have passed away, and all things have become new.' In the arms of Jesus a poor yet pardoned child had found rest. Not a cloud remained in all the sky to tell how the storm had raged, while the bow of promise spanned the entire horizon of my

being. Such was my conversion. It was entirely satis-
factory. Through all subsequent life I have never
had a doubt as to my full pardon and acceptance
with God."

The place, the spot, the hour where this wonderful
transformation took place was so photographed upon
her soul as ever to remain.

For years after she was in the habit of visiting that
church—if possible, on the anniversary of the night—
where, as the patriarch said, "The angels of God met
me." How many times have we heard her sing that
touching melody, composed by Dr. William Hunter,
expressive of her love for the sacred place:

> " There is a spot to me more dear
>   Than native vale or mountain;
> A spot for which affection's tear
>   Springs grateful from its fountain.
> 'Tis not where kindred souls abound,
>   'Though that is almost heaven,
> But where I first my Saviour found
>   And felt my sins forgiven.

> " Hard was my toil to reach the shore,
>   Long tossed upon the ocean;
> Above me was the thunder's roar,
>   Beneath, the waves' commotion.
> Darkly the pall of night was thrown
>   Around me, faint with terror;
> In that dark hour, how did my groan
>   Ascend for years of error.

"Sinking, and panting as for breath,
  I knew not help was near me;
I cried, 'O, save me, Lord, from death,
  Immortal Jesus, hear me!'
Then, quick as thought, I felt him mine;
  My Saviour stood before me;
I saw his brightness 'round me shine,
  And shouted, 'Glory! glory!'

"O sacred hour! O hallowed spot!
  Where love divine first found me;
Wherever falls my distant lot
  My heart shall linger 'round thee.
And when I rise from earth, and soar
  Up to my home in heaven,
Down will I cast my eyes once more
  Where I was first forgiven."

CHAPTER VIII.

Longing Desire to Tell Others.—Secret Prayer.—Joy in Parsonage.—Young Friend.—Strong Attachment.—Plighted Faith.—
Decline of Health.—Engagement Broken.—Triumphant Death.

IN this new life that so wonderfully opened to Nettie
it is not strange it should be followed by a longing
desire to tell it to others. When John Bunyan came
through that fearful conflict which he so graphically
describes in his *Pilgrim's Progress* he had such an
inlet of the love of God that "he felt he should swoon
for very joy;" "and I felt like telling the love of
God to the very crows in the field as I passed along."

It was real experience. Thousands have, since
David's day, taken up his testimony and said, "Come
unto me all ye that fear God, and I will declare what
he hath done for my soul." What was the substance
of God's doings? Completeness of pardon. "As far
as the east is from the west, so far hath he separated
my sins from me;" and he moreover declares, "I will
not hide thy righteousness in my heart." Let her
tell the story :

"Having passed out from the bondage and con-
demnation of sin, I felt a longing desire to tell it to

others. It was 'a fire in my bones,' and the joy I
experienced in telling it at home, among friends,
and in the sanctuary was beyond expression. The
most charming spot in my new life was the 'bower
of secret prayer.' There it seemed that heaven came
so near, and the dear Saviour communed with my in-
most being. I felt a love and longing for precious
souls. If God could accept my poor efforts in their
behalf they should be freely given. It was little I
might do, yet I could tell of Jesus. It was love overflowing and finding expression in simple language,
' Come to Jesus.' In this work I was personally blessed
and encouraged. To Christ be all the glory ; he gave
me precious souls. These are to me the richest treasures I possess ; they are worth far more than the
brightest gems of this perishing earth."

It was a joyful hour in that parsonage home—one
never to be forgotten. There was light in that dwelling then. Father, mother, friends rejoiced. All
praise to our loving Saviour! To Nettie it was the
supreme hour of her life. Her conversion had so
much of God and heaven in it as to forever leave it
out of Satan's power to lodge a temptation.

During her residence in Carlton Avenue there was
a young man engaged in the Marine Hospital that
frequently attended our church. He was a devoted
Christian and spent much of his time in religious

work, at the same time giving himself to study, as a preparation for the work of the ministry, to which he felt strongly called. Between Nettie and this Christian young man there sprang up a pleasant intimacy. His visits to the parsonage were frequent, until he became an acknowledged suitor.

His first work was performed under the presiding elder at Little Neck, Long Island. Here he labored with much success, organizing a society, which was soon blessed by a revival in which many were converted. His work culminated in building a neat and commodious church.

The following spring he was received as a probationer in the New York East Conference. With bright hopes he commenced what was supposed to be his life-work, and with his friends anticipated years of effective service. Their faith and love became plighted to each other. The life that now opened before her was in keeping with her fondest wishes. It would bring her into such relations with the Church as to afford her coveted opportunities for work in the cause of her Saviour.

He was a young man of good personal presence, of pleasing address, and winning manners; but more especially a devout child of God and deeply consecrated to the Master's service; while she whose recent religious experience had transformed her into a heavenly likeness only desired to live to honor her divine Lord.

In anticipation of the union of these two lives, so loving and devout, each seeking only to do the Master's will, it is not strange that mutual friends should believe it to be in accordance with the leadings of divine Providence.

During this year his health began to decline, and grave fears were entertained by many that his life was to be brief and he to become a victim of consumption. What increased the apprehension was, his mother had died of that dread disease when he was but an infant, entailing upon him by hereditary tendency the same fatal malady. He struggled and fought against it, and determined, if possible, to ward off the impending danger. He thought it wise to remove to the South as being a milder climate, thinking by this change he might overcome the disease that threatened his life.

Under these circumstances, with failing health and fears of an early death, what could Nettie do? What was her duty? To hold to her engagement to become the wife of one whose years would so soon terminate in death? It caused her deep anxiety and distress of mind.

In the fullness of her heart she carried the whole matter to God; she only prayed, "Lord, lead thou me and guide me." As a result it was thought best that the engagement should be broken. As against her fondest wishes this seemed to be the divine leading. If her hopes of a pleasant future were to be blighted, it was in the order of God, whose will she had come to feel as the only rule of her life. It cost them both a struggle, and the separation well-nigh overcame her. He went South and joined the Georgia Conference of the Methodist Episcopal Church, and was appointed to La Grange, in that State, where he labored during the year with great acceptability and some little apparent improvement to his health. The following spring he was transferred to the Baltimore Conference, and received an appointment within its bounds. At the ensuing Conference the question was asked: "What preachers have died this year?" Answer: "Only one death has occurred within the Conference during the year—Rev. Francis G. Kirby, a young and growing preacher, who died in holy triumph and went shouting to the land beyond the tide."

Thus passed away this truly excellent young minister before his sun had reached high noon—more than Nettie's friend—loved, respected, and regretted, to rest in "Abraham's bosom."

CHAPTER IX.

A New Enterprise.—Nettie's New Home.—Her Motto, "Must Jesus Bear the Cross Alone."—Enlarged Plans of Work.—Gift of Song.—A Vision.

IN the year 1864 several members of the DeKalb Avenue Methodist Episcopal Church, Brooklyn, started a mission in Tompkins Avenue, having for their pastor the Rev. Gad S. Gilbert, of the New York East Conference. For their temporary accommodation they erected a tabernacle, rudely constructed, where they worshiped. It was here, by this society, in the spring of 1865, that the pastor of Carlton Avenue Church was invited.

It became, therefore, Nettie's home for the next three years. While yet in her mother-church she had commenced to exercise her gifts in public. To do this was for her a great cross; naturally timid and diffident, it required the strong exercise of her will to undertake it. Her first efforts were very brief and simple, and sometimes would seem to be a failure. Nothing but her deep love for the Master, and a desire to help some struggling soul up the ladder or to win some poor one to the heart of Jesus, enabled her to continue this early cross-bearing. The power that moved her forward in this initial work is well explained in verses that often fell from her lips in song :

"Must Jesus bear the cross alone,
  And all the world go free ?
No ; there's a cross for every one,
  And there's a cross for me.

"The consecrated cross I'll bear,
  Till death shall make me free ;
And then go home, the crown to wear,
  For there's a crown for me."

She felt while bearing the cross that she was following the steps of her Saviour, who bore the cross for her, and she resolutely determined to "stand up for him."

Her testimony was simple, but all who listened saw her sincerity and earnestness. It was experience, out of her own heart. She would speak of the wonders of grace so that those who heard were convinced of the reality of the religion she professed, and their testimony was, "She has been with Jesus and learned of him."

Now, in her new church home in the tabernacle, she began to enlarge her plans of religious work. To her (as before noticed) was given the power of song, which in these later days has come to be recognized and acknowledged as a great factor in stirring human hearts. As long as she lived she used it as a power for good. Being a musician, she would usually accompany her music with song. With skilled fingers, with a soul inspired by the presence of the Holy Spirit, it is not strange that this heaven-endowed talent should be made a blessing to hundreds. She had, besides, a rich, musical voice of wonderful sweetness, and her words were spoken so clearly and distinctly that every expression could be heard and understood ; while often her face would be lighted up with a supernatural expression. These gave her labors more than ordinary interest and success. To this gift we shall have occasion to refer again.

In human lives there sometimes come points of interest the effects of which are felt through all future years. Such was Jacob's memorable experience at Beth-el. When he had laid himself down to sleep, with the heavens over him for a canopy, with a stone for his pillow, then there came the dream or vision. What he saw, heard, and felt so impressed itself upon his mind as to change and affect his whole future life.

About this time there was given to Nettie a similar vision or revelation. It impressed her deeply and affected her whole subsequent life. It was largely with her a pivotal hour. She sometimes referred to it in her ministrations, and always with subdued feelings and tearful eyes. We will let her speak of it herself:

5

A Vision.

"It was in the night season. On my bed I had a dream or vision. It appeared that my life had come to a close. My soul, dismissed from the body, was swiftly borne upward through the gates of the city.

"I saw things most beautiful. My very being was enraptured! As I passed along, accompanied by a heavenly one as my guide, I came to a place most beautifully fitted up, in which I saw a large number of robes, bright and beautiful, and very many crowns. I turned to my guide, and said, 'Here among these is my robe and crown, let me take and wear them.' He replied, 'You can have them.' I soon found them; I knew they were mine; I put on the robe, and it seemed to be made for me, and my crown fitted my brow. But as I looked at them I was disappointed and deeply affected. I said to my guide, 'This is my crown and robe, but see! there are some spots on this robe, and I want mine to be a *spotless robe;* this crown is my crown, but there are no stars in it; I don't want to wear a *starless crown.'*

"My guide took them from me and said, 'If such be your desire, go back to yonder world, my child, and live and work for your Master, and when your robe shall become spotless and your crown studded with stars, then you shall come again and take and wear them.'"

What a revelation was this to her. From that time her highest ambition seemed to be to accomplish and make complete the prophetic vision. "A spotless robe" and a "crown full of stars" was what she lived and labored for. It was ever the voice of God ringing through her soul, and intensified her longing for the salvation and uplifting of others, and it often found the following expression : "Who would be willing to think when dying, my life has been fruitless—nothing but leaves ; I have done nothing for Jesus, and see only in reserve a starless crown."

CHAPTER X.

Sabbath-school Work.—Home, Its Help and Cheer.—A New Gift to the Pastor's Home.—Nettie's Joy and Thanksgiving.—A Brother's Greeting.—Her Hopes.—Labors Blessed.

IN her Tompkins Avenue church-home Nettie gathered around her a large class of young ladies in the Sabbath-school. She became their teacher and instructor. She took them each and laid them on her heart. It was not enough that the ordinary exercises of the school were employed—her loving, longing soul would not be satisfied until those dear ones of the class were led to the Saviour. The most of them were converted and united with the church.

We have already spoken of her love for home. Never did parents possess a richer treasure than they had in this their daughter. In the home-circle her presence was a benediction. She was the affectionate child, a loving sister, and a companion and helper to both father and mother. In some peculiar trials her father was here called to meet she entered into sympathy with him, and by her cheerful words and loving presence became a support and strength to him.

And this was characteristic of all her life. To her

father she was a "helper in the Gospel." With no one did she so much delight to labor and work as with him, and he always felt support and encouragement when she was by his side. Sometimes a failure in a sermon, or what appeared to be a useless effort, would, when Nettie came to the rescue, be turned from defeat into victory. Next to her Saviour she leaned on her father, and he quite as much depended upon her for success. And it is our strong conviction that in those gracious revivals that followed at Tompkins Avenue, Rockville Center, Jamaica, and elsewhere, in which hundreds were saved, Nettie was a large and important factor.

It was here, in the month of May, 1867, that another gift came to the pastor's family in the form of a little babe—the first and only boy. In that home this was a joyful event, and none was more delighted than Nettie.

When that little infant was placed in her arms it seemed as if her cup of joy was full to overflowing, and, kneeling down with eyes filled with tears of gladness, she praised the Lord for the gift. There was a large place in her heart for that little brother—she received him as a gift from God—whose coming filled her cup to the brim. How warm and intense her love for him; how solicitous for his welfare through all the years of her life, growing stronger as he grew in years, knowing no diminution up to the hour when her death made the separation.

Perhaps the following lines might more properly belong to the family than to the public, but as they breathe forth her deep sisterly affection we cannot refrain from giving them a place in this memorial:

To My Brother.—Greeting.

O, well do I remember, boy,
　　When first you came to town ;
When in your mother's arms you lay
　　In flannel-slip and gown.

Your bright and shining eyes,
　　And round and chubby face ;
As if an angel from the skies
　　Held you in his embrace.

How soft and white your little feet,
　　And little dimpled knees ;
But, O, our joy was not complete
　　Until we heard you sneeze.

A name we for our darling sought,
　　In books and spellers old ;
But not in one that could be brought,
　　The baby's name unfold.

The mother spoke in tones of joy,
　　Upon conditions, this :
If ever I should have a boy
　　His name is Clinton Fisk.

His slips and bands are laid aside
  For trowsers bright and new ;
While in the apple bough he rides
  Full many a journey through.

The hobby-horse has run his race,
  The train of cars are still ;
While in the school he takes his place,
  And waits his teacher's will.

The tide of life is sweeping on,
  With scarce a halt between ;
The little boy has now become
  A youth of full sixteen.

May heaven guide my own sweet one,
  My baby boy and love,
Out from the nest of father's home
  To that sweet home above.

In a letter written home about this time she tells of having attended church in an adjoining village, and listening to a sermon from a young minister. One of the chords touched by that sermon, that vibrated through her heart, may be seen from the following extract :

" O, how much would I love to have my own dear brother become a minister when he comes to manhood. I trust I may live to see the day when I shall sit in the congregation and hear him preach the word of life. My heart goes out in prayer to God, that he may follow in the footsteps of his and my dear father and preach the blessed Gospel."

A very gracious revival occurred in Tompkins Avenue. A large and beautiful church had been built, taking the place of the rude tabernacle which had answered its day. For nearly a year it had been occupied by a growing congregation. During the last six months of the pastor's stay God had " visited his people," and a goodly number were added. In that work our dear Nettie bore a conspicuous part. Among the young people the Lord greatly blessed her labors, and her gifts were enlarged only to be renewedly consecrated to the Lord's service. The separation of the pastor and his family from this church home was one of the incidents of our itinerant life. It severed hearts and lives that had been cemented together by blessings and sorrows, by discipline and trial.

None shared more largely in these experiences than Nettie, and there was a deep, wide-spread sorrow when she went out from their midst.

CHAPTER XI.

Jamaica Her Home for Three Years.—Stepping Forth in a New Field.—Experience of Entire Sanctification.—Special Laborers in the Field.—Holiness Convention.—Her Experience.—Father Obtains the Blessing.—Work Commences in the Church.—Temptations.—Oakington.—Witness Received Through the Blood.

"JAMAICA" fell from the lips of the presiding bishop at the Conference of 1869, in connection with the name of the pastor removing from Tompkins Avenue. This was Nettie's next home for three years, and, if we may except Carlton Avenue, was of all places most dearly identified with her religious life and experience.

A removal to a new home, to be surrounded by a new people, has in many instances proved detrimental to religious progress, especially to the young. It requires more courage and resolution to keep up the standard of religious habits than when among those we know and love. But no change of place or people caused her to halt or weary for a single moment. As the Lord opened her way she stepped forth with all the zeal of her renewed nature, and began to work for God and immortal souls. For six years she had been walking in the light of justification, having "peace with God through our Lord Jesus Christ," and, like her divine Lord, "going about doing good." These were years that knew no backsliding, no halting in her heavenward journey. She truly loved the Lord, and delighted in his service. So with a loving heart, with much prayer and "singing for Jesus," she commenced her work in the church and village of Jamaica. How quickly and warmly she won hearts here to herself need not be told. Friends multiplied, while her own heart expanded and took them all in.

Besides her home duties—for she was never idle, assuming a share of the household work, assisting mother, caring for Dollie, the dear sister, now a girl of nine years of age, and "my precious boy," as she was wont to speak of him—she had a large class of pupils to whom she gave lessons on the piano and organ. This brought her in contact with a large number of families outside of the church, so that her acquaintance and influence became extended. Her life and deportment were such that she had "a good report from them that were without."

We approach now a time—a most deeply interesting period—when she entered more fully into an everlasting covenant with God, "ordered in all things and sure," when she sought and obtained the blessing of "entire sanctification," in the light and beauty of which she walked for nineteen years, until her translation to that immortal life beyond.

Here with God's people, with whom she went out and in, and to her most intimate friends, there appeared no halting in the religious race, no waning interest in the service of Christ, and no abatement of her love for souls. It was not in her case, as sometimes is alleged of others, that this new experience was a "new start," or a "recovery from heart-wanderings and backslidings." It came to her when she enjoyed not only "reconciliation with God," but "peace through our Lord Jesus Christ."

This gracious work—so full, so wide-reaching—experienced by her may well be related at length, for we think "herein our Father in heaven is glorified." It was the crown jewel set in the diadem of her experience, when, as never before, she rose to the full stature of an elect one in Christ Jesus.

From this wondrous hour her life flowed on more beautifully than ever. Her faith experienced a wider stretch and power, and her harp of song was keyed up to notes never reached before.

When God comes to an individual or a people he usually prepares the way. So to this dear one there came the preparation—the "day-star from on high"—until the Sun of Righteousness arose full orbed in her soul.

The subject of "entire sanctification" as a dis-

tinct blessing to be received by faith, and now, was
not very largely preached by our ministers. The
Church was exhorted to "go on from grace to grace,"
and that God's people might have "all the religion
they would live for." That seemed to be about the
measure of the average preaching of the times.
Preachers claimed to preach "entire sanctification"
and "heart holiness," but it was mostly based upon
the idea of "growth." Every preacher among us had
declared at the bar of his Conference that "he expected to be made perfect in love in this life;" and
in answer to the question, "Are you earnestly groan-
ing for it?" would answer in the affirmative; but
how little was the clear, emphatic declaration sounded
out from the pulpit: "It is the will of God, even
your sanctification"—now, by faith—enforced by
the encouraging words, "Faithful is He that calleth
you, who also will do it." Hence but seldom did
God's dear children come into the clear witness of
perfect love. Such testimonies were rare in the
churches. There had, however, commenced a revival upon the subject of holiness. God had raised
up special witnesses to this blessed truth. That evangelist of precious memory, Mrs. Phebe Palmer, and a
few others, were declaring God's truth upon this subject with no uncertain sound, and the precious leaven
was spreading.

How much opposition it met in the churches and by ministers need not be told. It is a matter of history. Wonderful in development and results were the experience and preaching of the Rev. John S. Inskip. The blessing was first experienced by his loving wife; then came to him one who touched his lips with Isaiah's burning coal; then, with all the force and power of his redeemed nature, he took it up and sounded it out, " O Zion, put on thy beautiful garments." How the work spread, and how the churches were thrilled by this new incoming of heavenly light has become a matter of history.

About this time the "National Camp-meeting for the Promotion of Holiness" was born. Many doubted, some ridiculed, while there were not wanting those that " waited for the consolation of Israel," and were fervently praying, " Let thy kingdom come."

And the kingdom did come, and preachers commenced to fall into line, and by a new and higher experience themselves began to press the subject upon their people, and declare that even *now*, by faith, they might enter into the font of cleansing.

This was the prepared way to Nettie. The dawning of the day was near at hand; the rays of light were being crystallized, and fell in brightness upon her open and receptive heart. We desire to let her in her own words furnish us with that experience. She says :

"As the years of my life sweetly glided along this joy remained" (alluding to her justification and subsequent experience). "Ever and anon richer baptisms fell upon my soul. The great desire uppermost was *work for the Master*. I was not satisfied unless I was conscious of progress in religious experience. I loved Jesus more, and I felt I had rather die than leave him. This was my experience when I was called to a fuller consecration than ever before. At times I feared my affections were not supremely his, and this was a grief to me. Then there came a longing of heart to be all the Lord's.

"How strange that with such desires I should object to the Bible term, 'entire sanctification.' Somehow when I heard this word used it did not find a pleasant response in my heart. I wanted the grace, but disliked the term. Those meetings where the subject of sanctification was made a specialty became distasteful to me. I now recall those feelings and wonder. They appear strange and unaccountable.

"About this time my father attended a national camp-meeting at Round Lake. He returned the following week. As he entered the house, after the greetings were over, I saw something in his look and manner that impressed me. I said, 'Ma, father has received the blessing.' I knew it; and, sure enough, he had; for he lovingly declared it to us all and in public that the blood of Jesus Christ, his Son, had cleansed him from all sin. During the subsequent months of the year he not only preached it, but it was manifest in his life. He breathed it in his prayers; he confessed it with his tongue. A sacred influence seemed to surround him in our home. O, how carefully I watched my dear father, for I saw in him what my soul longed for. It was heart-purity in the life.

"In him I saw it; my prejudices were fast melting away under this new and living exhibition of holiness, while there took hold of my heart an intense desire for the same precious grace. I attended meetings held by father and elsewhere for the promotion of holiness. At these meetings, when the invitation would be given to come forward as a definite seeker for 'entire sanctification,' my heart would rise in strange rebellion. I would gladly go as a seeker for 'a deeper work of grace' or 'more religion' or even for a 'clean heart.'

"But the conviction was laid so heavy upon my heart that it could not be suppressed or stifled. The Holy Ghost had put the cry within me, 'Create in me a clean heart.' But I wanted to dictate the terms. If I could get the divine filling and keep sanctification out of sight all would go well; but God held me to his own terms, and there rang through my soul these words, '*Sanctify* them through thy truth.' If you will accept the doctrine of entire sanctification, so far you will be in accord with God's will; for 'this is the will of God, even your sanctification.'

"About this time, with my dear father and some friends from our church, I attended the National Camp-meeting held at Oakington, Md. Here I found the burden of preaching, the prayers, and songs were 'sanctification.' The old controversy for a time struggled for supremacy. But God had led me to this place, and his light was shining through my heart. A voice seemed to speak to me: 'Will you receive Christ as your perfect Saviour? Will you accept him *now* by faith, giving your whole being to him in a full consecration forever?' I know not why it was, but my heart failed to respond, when for the first time since my conversion a great darkness came over me, and every ray of light seemed to be withdrawn. My conscious enjoyment was removed. I felt I had grieved the blessed Spirit who had presented for my acceptance the priceless pearl I had refused. Yet amid that darkness I still loved my Saviour; my heart still clung to him, and I felt I would die before I would leave him. Just at this point the Spirit helped me to yield. I said, I will accept Christ with all the terms; yes, even as ' my sanctifier.' Another temptation came, for I had to contend every step I made; it was this: 'Suppose the blessing should come and you should lose your strength—suppose you should shout and make a noise—are you willing to take it just as God shall be pleased to send it?' A little more shrinking just as the prize was being grasped. But the blessed Spirit helped me, and my trembling soul said: 'Any way, Lord, only fully save; let it be "entire sanctification,"' for I was steadily held to that point. In this extremity, in my tent near the midnight hour, my stubborn will yielding, the last plank upon which I stood gone, there came over my soul '*the cleansing wave.*' I was *fully* saved—*sanctified*—filled. The all-atoning blood had now done its work, and I was henceforth and forever the Lord's. O, that wondrous hour! the sweetest of all my life. The word that so long had been a stone of stumbling now appeared the most beautiful in all the language.

"I found it meant so much; it awakened harmonies in my soul beyond description. Oblivious to all surroundings I shouted in that midnight hour, '*I have it! I have it!*' Like the dawning of heaven the day had broken upon me. For hours my soul reveled in a bliss far beyond my largest imagination, the cross in beauty arose before me, glittering as with a thousand diamonds, encircled by the word 'Sanctification,' and the little tent became radiant—it seemed full of light—while the angels of God appeared to

6

hover over the scene breathing their celestial music upon my soul. A cloud of glory filled the place. It was Jesus whom through the hours I had 'held, but could not see.' Now he had 'knighted me on the field.' As a prince I had 'wrestled and prevailed.' I had come into such union with Jesus that I could understand the meaning of those words hitherto but partially comprehended, 'I in them and thou in me.'

"Such perfect rest; my heart believed as naturally as I breathed. And faith brought rest, for 'they which do believe have entered unto rest.' So I sang:

> " 'No storm can move this inward rest,
>   While to that refuge clinging ;
> All things are mine since I am his,
>   How can I keep from singing !' "

CHAPTER XII.

HAVRE DE GRACE.—CONSECRATION.—VERSES.—BEULAH LAND.—TES-
TIMONY OF J. C. ACKER.—EYE-WITNESSES.—TARRYING AT JERUSALEM.
—REVIVAL AT JAMAICA.—VICTORY.—APPOINTED CLASS-LEADER.—
OVER THE RIVER.

BEFORE returning from Oakington in company
with some friends she visited for a few hours the
village or city of Havre de Grace. While here sitting
on the banks of the broad and beautiful Susquehanna
she writes as follows, on July 18, 1870 :

" Here I give myself wholly to Jesus. How fully
I am saved.

" ' O, glorious hope of perfect love !
It lifts me up to things above ;
It bears on eagles' wings.'

" Before me flows gently and quietly this beautiful
river ; dotted here and there by boats of various kind,
so this day my little bark is gliding out on the ocean
of redeeming love, while at my feet breaks the blessed
waves of salvation. Upon this prominence I sit. I see
on either side the beautiful verdure, the trees lifting
themselves up as if joining the universal chorus of
song to the great Creator. But far more beautiful to
me are the green pastures and verdant fields through

which he leads me to-day. A song of glory arises from my heart to God and the Lamb. I listen and hear the birds sing, and the song finds an echo through my soul. I seem to see Jesus as he sat beside the quiet lake of Gennesaret and taught and fed the multitude. So his words are to-day food to my soul; and as when out upon that lake the storm had burst and the disciples were greatly afraid he arose and spoke, ' Peace, be still,' so he speaks to my inward consciousness, and a sweet stillness falls upon me."

In regard to this wonderful experience Nettie wrote as follows:

" After four years have passed since the above was written I have but to repeat it over and over and to adore my blessed Lord. The half has never yet been told, for with added years have come richer joys and experience, and added glory!

" I am tasting the riper fruits of this earthly Canaan. While my soul digs deeper and finds richer treasures in his word, heaven seems to come nearer, and so I stand on these mortal shores as victor, and fully adopt the rich language of Charles Wesley's hymn:

" ' Lame as I am, I take the prey;
   Hell, earth, and sin, with ease o'ercome;
I leap for joy, pursue my way,
   And as a bounding hart fly home,
 Through all eternity to prove
 Thy nature and thy name is Love.' "

About this time her newly consecrated and sanctified soul, luxuriating in the sunlight of heaven, describes still farther her feelings in the following verses
composed by her:

"HOW CAN I KEEP FROM SINGING?

"I go to Jesus when I'm weak,
   I ask for strength to help me ;
I hear the precious promise speak,
   Draw near, and I will help thee.
I see the glory of my Lord
   While at the cross I'm kneeling ;
I'm washed and cleansed in Jesus' blood—
   How can I keep from singing ?

"In plenteous showers I feel it now,
   With joy my soul is beaming ;
While at his feet I'm bending low
   I feel the glory streaming.
I find it in the quiet rest,
   My soul on God is leaning;
O, here I am so sweetly blest—
   How can I keep from singing ?

"The joy and light that fills my soul,
   The land of Beulah seeming ;
With corn and milk, with wine and oil,
   This goodly land is teeming.
The birds—they sing the whole year round,
   No winter checks their hymning ;
With every joy it doth abound—
   How can I keep from singing ?

> " I taste the honey from the rock,
>   With love my cup is flowing ;
> He says, ' I lead my little flock
>   Where pastures green are growing.'
> Beside the waters pure and still
>   My gentle Guide is leading ;
> With perfect love my soul doth fill—
>   How can I keep from singing ? "

She had indeed reached the Beulah land where the birds sang day and night and the sun never went down. Such a joy was hers that it became a "fire in her bones," or as an overflowing peace that ran over the banks and refreshed those around her. She could not refrain from telling it. As the blessed Spirit touched the chords of her soul, it gave forth notes of the purest and sweetest melody.

We cannot refrain from giving place to a brief paper sent to us by request from Brother J. C. Acker, who was at the time of this experience Nettie's class-leader. He and his excellent wife were among the few that attended the Oakington camp-meeting with Nettie :

" An Item in the Experience of Nettie Hill.

"In the summer of 1869 her father, Rev. Francis C. Hill, then pastor of the Methodist Episcopal church in Jamaica, attended the Round Lake National Camp-meeting for the Promotion of Holiness. While there he entered into the experience of entire sanctification.

Upon returning home to his charge he preached the doctrine and testified to the experience. He awakened quite an interest as well as opposition to the subject.

"At this time Nettie was not in full sympathy with the doctrine; but her confidence in her father prevented her speaking against the experience, though at times she was much exercised in regard to the matter. The next summer (1870) she attended the National Camp-meeting at Oakington, Md.

"When there the blessed Holy Spirit applied the truth, and such deep conviction came to her heart that she felt as though she had lost all her religion. She presented herself as a seeker after heart-purity— she did not like the word 'sanctification.' For about three days she passed through a deep struggle before she was able and willing to surrender fully, and take Christ by faith alone as her complete Saviour.

"For several hours so severe was the conflict that her strength was gone, yet she was unsatisfied; she had not received the fullness that she sought and that she had heard others testify. There was a calm, quiet rest —a consciousness of full consecration—and as far as she knew she was 'all the Lord's.' This state continued for two days, until on Tuesday night, after the meetings had closed for the day, her tent's company spent some time in talking over the events of the day and their experience (for all were seeking for holiness), and then engaged in family worship. Each of the little company in turn led in prayer, when the presence of the Master was so manifest that they felt that they were in the very presence of God; so precious was the communion, so divine the fellowship, that prayer was continued I know not how long, until it became lost in praise and shouts of joy, of glory, and victory. This awoke the people from their sleep in the adjoining tents, and the Holy Ghost came upon them in mighty power. Our tent was filled with his visible glory—a light so pure, so white—a glory indescribable —light without a shadow.

"A vision was given to Nettie at this hour of the glorified Saviour floating in space with the word 'sanctification' above him in letters of fire, and she exclaimed, '"Sanctification," the sweetest word I ever heard or saw.' Ever after she had a special love for scriptural terms, and continued to testify to the end of her life that the 'Lord had sanctified her throughout body, soul, and spirit.'"

It is pleasant to record the above, coming from an eye-witness of that blessed experience. In conversations had with those dear friends upon the subject they speak of it as being the most remarkable occasion they ever witnessed. The glory that shone down into that little tent was not only felt in the soul, but that it was visible to the senses they ever have declared. It was, indeed, as the mount of transfiguration, where the disciples of old beheld his glory; so they declare and firmly believe. From that hour not only were the richest blessings received, but results far-reaching followed.

Until now Nettie's work had been principally within her own church. She had "tarried at Jerusalem" until the divine "enduement" came; then her enlarged soul looked for other and wider fields of labor, and the Master of the vineyard opened them to her—not a few. In the Methodist Episcopal church a remarkable revival of holiness had commenced a few months before. More than two-score of the members had "entered into this valley of blessing so sweet," and the work continued to go on. A deeply interesting meeting of two days was held in the church led by that saintly woman, Mrs. Phebe Palmer, and her devoted husband, Dr. Palmer. Now that Nettie had come out such a clear and positive witness the work increased and multiplied; for as from her early Christian experience she did not "hide God's righteousness in her heart," even more now did she stand forth as a witness of full salvation.

During the following winter a meeting was appointed in the church nightly, which continued about eight weeks. In this meeting Nettie was deeply interested.

It called out her strongest and best efforts. The apparent delay (for weeks passed before a break occurred) tested her faith in common with others. But she never wavered nor doubted. "The Lord is coming," she would say, and her unyielding faith was an inspiration to the pastor as well as others. She with God's dear people became more and more drawn out for the conversion of sinners and closer to God in holy consecration.

With the law that governs revivals we are not disposed to speculate. The KEY that unlocks God's storehouse and brings the times of refreshing we think is largely found in the word, " Ye shall seek me, and find me, when ye shall *search* for me with all your heart."

It appeared specially true in this instance. The church waited on God not only in prayer, but in Christian activity. The people were invited and urged to come to the feast. Earnest ones went out into the highways and hedges and tenderly compelled them to come. One special instance may be mentioned. Mr. J. B. Hopkins had lately been received by letter from the Dutch Reformed Church. His heart had become newly touched, and his love glowed and burned with furnace heat. Brother Hopkins resided at Jamaica, south, about four miles from the church. His manner was to harness his team to his large market-wagon, then to go around the neighborhood and gather up the friends, especially the unconverted, and bring them to the church. This he did night after night for six weeks, through wind and rain or snow, with the intermission of a single night. Out of twenty-six persons brought almost nightly to the church twenty-five gave good evidence of being soundly converted. These all came into the church. A vigorous and growing class was appointed, with Brother Hopkins for its leader. Many of these soon became the acknowledged witnesses of the all-cleansing blood to save from sin.

With such "working faith" and "laboring love" as witnessed here it is no marvel that God came and victory was given to the Lord's dear ones. The altar was thronged nightly by seeking penitents, while an awful sense of the divine presence rested upon the people. Awakenings multiplied; convictions were deep; strong men and women were smitten with an unseen power, and fell to the floor as if slain in battle. The number of the converted increased, while new witnesses of perfect love were multiplied.

In such a time as this we may imagine what a part our dear one occupied. She was a force and inspiration. If she was not *the* leader she was one of the captains that led her hundreds, whose songs, prayers, and exhortations were heard all along the line helping many into the kingdom, and not a few over the Jordan into the goodly land of perfect love. There was appointed to her a large class of young converts; she became their leader. By her loving instructions and prayers they all continued steadfast, and a large part came soon in their Christian experience into the enjoyment of "full salvation." It could hardly be otherwise; she who was their guide and counselor walked and lived before them as a pattern of holiness. They often heard from her lips, "Let us go on to perfection," while with sweet encouragement she declared, "Faithful is he who hath called you, who also will do it;" and as they looked into her face and heard her say,

> "Let us at once go up,
> No more on this side of Jordan stop,"

many responded, "We will." Thus they followed their leader into the "greener pastures" of Christian experience. When the months of their probation passed there had been no losses. Every one stood at the altar as a candidate for full membership. Among these converts was David J. Weeden, who afterward became her husband. He also during the following year experienced the blessing of "entire sanctification," and has since without abatement walked in the light of this grace. As an exhibit of her own experience at this time the following hymn and tune were composed by her and often sung:

Sweetly Resting.

Words and Music by Miss NETTIE HILL.

1. My all I give to thee, O Sav-iour, make me thine;
2. Re-flect thy life in me, Thy poor, un-wor-thy one;

Thine im-age in me see, From sin and dross re-fine.
My bod-y, let it be The tem-ple of thy Son.

CHORUS.

Oh, then I'm rest-ing In a Sav-iour's love;

Yes, yes, I'm trust-ing In the pre-cious blood.

3 My heart and thoughts renew,
  By thine all-cleansing blood;
Make me entirely new,
  Bathed in the crimson flood.

4 I give my life to thee;
  Use it as seemeth best;
But Jesus, make me free,
  In thee alone be blest.

5 Receive the offering now,
  And save me from above;
'Tis done! my heart I bow:
  I'm filled with perfect love.

6 Hail, blessèd Holy Ghost,
  Who sweetly makes us free'
Restores thine image, lost;
  The fullness now to me.

CHAPTER XIII.

BEFORE closing the record of Nettie's experience
and labors at Jamaica we desire to mention the
young people's meetings commenced and carried forward by her work and labor of love. Concerning
this she writes:

"During the revival of 1870–1 in our church
many were gathered into the fold under the ministry
of my dear father. With these, especially the young,
I was brought into very close and sweet fellowship.
A deep impression seemed to be laid upon me to do
something more to aid and strengthen them, and to
hold them together in their new spiritual life. I sought
to bring them into a fuller consecration to Christ and
encourage them to labor for the salvation of others.

"As to what were the best methods I thought much,
and earnestly asked the Lord to help me. I soon obtained the assurance I sought and, following the leadings of the blessed Spirit, went forward.

"I invited the young people to meet me at the par-

sonage. Ten of those dear ones responded to the call.
At that meeting new courage was given me for future
work. Subsequently, every week this little band met
together, while their numbers continued to increase
until the class-room of the chapel became too small
for us, and the room was often filled not only with
people, but with the glory of God. Often such man-
ifestations of divine grace would be realized, such
earnest prayers, such loving exhortations, such praise,
from these young Christians, as to gladden all hearts."

"But in her duty, prompt at every call,
She watched and wept, she prayed and felt for all ;
And as a bird each fond endearment tries
To tempt its new-fledged offspring to the skies,
She tried each art, reproved each dull delay,
Allured to brighter worlds, and led the way."

Thus the year passed on. During that time many
of these young Christians, and some older ones, entered into the experience of "perfect love." There
were some that strongly opposed ; still, the work went
on, for it was of the Lord. New ones were converted
and sanctifications were multiplied. It was not an
uncommon thing to see God's people lose their strength
and become prostrated by the wondrous power of God.

Among the converts and members of that meeting
were Demott Remsen, Anna Snedeker, Sarah Hull,
Emma Remsen, Sadie Morrell, Libbie Rider, Frank
Wood, Sadie Baylis, and Tany Remson. These

enjoyed the sweet fellowship of that meeting, and ripened for a higher union before the throne. Remaining steadfast, they each ran a good race and finished their course with joy, and have gone to their bright crowning in the land beyond.

But these times of refreshing so delightful came to a close. The great itinerant wheel took up the pastor's family and landed it elsewhere in the Lord's vineyard. The questions were asked, "Who will care for these dear young people?" "Who will shepherd this little flock now?" Brother Mortimer Wood was chosen, and for his assistant Sister Martie Baylis, now the excellent wife of Rev. A. C. Bowdish, of the New York East Conference. Faithful in his devotion and labor of love, for seventeen years was Brother Wood found through winter and summer, sunshine and storm, at this meeting commenced by Nettie.

Many changes have taken place; the young have become older, while those whose names we have recorded with her who started the work, who used to sing so sweetly the "Old, old story," have exchanged it for the "New, new song."

The parting of the pastor and family from the Jamaica charge was a sorrowful one. To Nettie it was deeply felt, and her removal was regretted by the church. They could have a new pastor—one who could take the place of the retiring one—the loss could be made good; but the almost universal feeling through church and community was that no one could be found to fill her place. Aside from her immediate class she had, as stated by her, organized a meeting for six o'clock on Sunday evening, which was continued for seventeen years, and was yet in vigorous operation when she died.

No wonder her presence would be missed, and that there should be sorrow at her parting; but the light of this bright star as it temporarily set upon this dear church and people arose to shine in another part of God's vineyard.

For the next three years the parsonage in Johnson Street, Brooklyn, was her home, and the church largely the field of her Christian work and devotion.

Here in her new home the people were not long in finding out this fact—that a pure-hearted Christian and a willing worker had come into their midst. Her first Christian labor here gave no uncertain sound. Her religious testimony was strong and clear and the people were won to her. She avouched her love for the Master by confessing him as her full and complete Saviour. She hesitated not to lift up a standard that "the blood of Jesus Christ, his Son, does cleanse from all sin." This, added to her consistent and holy life, gave power and efficiency to her profession. Here, as elsewhere, a large class of young ladies was placed

7

under her charge in the Sabbath-school. She tenderly loved them, and by her deep and earnest devotion had the happiness of seeing the most of them converted and become members of the church.

While at Johnson Street, during the third year she was united to David J. Weeden in holy marriage. He who now became her husband was converted to God in Jamaica, and the year following obtained the clear witness of perfect love. God had made her largely instrumental in all this. On February 13, 1874, these two lives were united, henceforth to walk in the pathway of life ; to journey together to the heavenly country. This sweet mystic union continued nearly sixteen years, until "she was not, for God had translated her." The following was taken from the village paper :

"Marriage Ceremony.

"On Wednesday last Miss Nettie Hill, daughter of the Rev. Francis C. Hill, formerly pastor of the Methodist Episcopal church of our village, and Mr. David J. Weeden, well known to all our villagers, did the very best possible thing that a happy and loving couple could do. They joined their hands together in the solemn bonds of wedlock, and started out to share the joys and blessings of life, and to meet with mutual strength whatever storms might come.

"They were married in Brooklyn, in the Johnson

NETTIE WHEN MARRIED—TWENTY-NINE YEARS OF AGE.

Street Methodist Episcopal Church, of which the bride's father is pastor, the ceremony being performed by her father, assisted by the Rev. R. C. Putney, of our village, and the Rev. J. E. Searles, of the Washington Street Church.

"The bridesmaids were Miss Anna Fosdic and Miss Frances E. Hill, a sister of the bride. Mr. Edward F. Titus, of this village, and Mr. John L. Baker, of Greenport, acted the part of groomsmen; all doing their part in a manner that won the encomiums of all present. The church was crowded with the interested friends of the couple, a large number of ladies and gentlemen from our village being among them.

"The bride's Sabbath-school class was present in a body, and in all the exuberance and joy of the occasion plainly showed with what deep regret they separated from her.

"The bride is a cultivated and amiable lady, having many warm friends here where she has taken up her new home, and the best wishes greet her and her happy husband in the new life they have entered upon. We tender our heartiest congratulations."

This was an event in which the church, both at Johnson Street and at Jamaica, seemed to be deeply interested. They somehow as by adoption claimed her as their own, and tears of joy and congratulations were poured out freely from all.

CHAPTER XIV.

Returns to Jamaica.—The Open Door.—Her Presence and Labors Missed.—Removes to Huntington.—Recollections by Rev. E. Warrinner.

FOR a time the residence of the newly wedded pair was at Jamaica, where she returned after an absence of three years to set up a new home in the place of her father's; but as she for a time went out from under the "family tree," she still retained all her warmest love and attachment for that home. She suffered no abatement of interest or affection even to life's latest hour. In an article written by her eighteen years since, and published in the *Christian Woman*, she very strongly emphasizes this:

"Influence of Home.

"As starlight rises into sunlight, as darkness into brightness, so should the radiance of heart-purity be exemplified in home life, *a home shining* of the precious Gospel, a millennial dawning around the family altar, the bow of promise, a fiery pillar to guide that circle to the skies. Such a purity throws a mantle of light over every step in life, and paints with artistic fingers each somber cloud with the rich tinge of complete trust in Jesus. It takes the frosted and withered flowers of earth, and draws therefrom the fragrance of joy and love.

"Such a purity chases away the ice and sleet of winter, and bids the child of earthly birth go and bathe in the fountain of life and cleansing, where, instead of a life of bondage and servitude, the blessed freedom of the *child*, the *son*, the *daughter*, the *heir* is completely enjoyed. How sweetly, then, is realized the prophet's vision : 'For ye shall go out with joy, and be led forth with peace, and the mountains and hills shall break forth before you into singing, and all the trees of the field shall clap their hands.'

"In such a home Jesus dwelt. It was this that invested that little home in Bethany with such a strange beauty. It is because of such a home that the writer of this article to-day enjoys the sweet, perfect rest of faith. Not gathered into the fold by the voice of the stranger, not an exotic planted by foreign hands, but grown under the influence of home culture. It was here at the family hearthstone that the ingrafted word was received.

"Not all the solemn exhortations or the victorious songs of God's dear host could do what was done by the quiet but telling eloquence of home.

"The streamlet that ever flows on in sweetness

must have its source.   Higher than the stream is the fountain.

"That fountain I found to be Jesus, and trusting in him entirely he is my *present* and *complete* Saviour.

"And when at the last others shall swell the vast train and chant their victories for Jesus, be it enough for me to stand among the adoring throng and say, Here am I, washed in the precious blood, brought thither through the influence of home, and, with the dear ones that have won me for glory, receive the victor's crown.

"Then, while others sing their anthems to Jesus, and joyfully mention the names of those who were instrumental in bringing them there, I will strike a sweeter chord, will raise a higher note, that methinks will vibrate through all the shining realms of bliss— *my earthly home opened for me the golden gates of heaven!*

> "My boast is not that I derive my birth
> From loins enthroned, and rulers of the earth ;
> But higher far my proud pretensions rise,
> The child of parents going to the skies."

In her return she was warmly welcomed by the community and former friends, who gathered around her, giving her the assurance of their love and esteem.

"Behold, I set before thee an open door which no man can shut."   These were words spoken to one of the seven churches; often they come to individuals. To Nettie they came; to her there was an open door, and through it she walked forth to toil and work for the Master.

Meanwhile her father was appointed by his Conference to Rockville Center, L. I. This was the first move the pastor and family had made without Nettie's help and presence. It appeared strange, and to a degree unpleasant, to go to a new people and a new charge without her. To enter upon the new work in the vineyard and she absent seemed almost a bereavement.

For so many years she had been a cheer and inspiration in the family circle; she had become more than a child—a companion, a helper—to both father and mother. Now, in the public service the pastor missed her radiant face, and in the prayer-meeting her voice in testimony and prayer was wanting. Perhaps he had come to depend too much upon her. As to this God only knows.

That she should for a time leave her home seemed to be in the order of providence; but her visits were frequent, and her life-long interest in her father and his work brought her often to his help. Especially was this the case in a revival that commenced in the fall and continued on until winter, when more than one hundred souls professed to find pardon, the most of whom united with the church.

About this time she and her husband removed to
the village of Huntington, where for about five years
they lived and labored. This brought her to the birthplace of her father and the scene of the labors of her
sainted grandmother, whose voice for many years had
been silent in death. That Nettie should come to live
and labor in the same society seemed to be a striking
coincidence. But so it was ; and there were those yet
living who remembered the spirit and work of the
first, that saw them duplicated by the second.

In olden times there were those that said of Christ,
when they saw his work and heard of his fame, "This
is John the Baptist; he is risen from the dead ; and
therefore mighty works do show forth themselves in
him." So it appeared as if the grandmother had again
returned to earth to be seen in the living labors of the
grandchild.

Here in her new home her voice was heard in prayer
and testimony. She at once unfurled the flag and
"lifted up a standard." Her house was opened,
weekly meetings were appointed and held, and the
presence of the Lord was made manifest to her and
the people.

Soon after her death, by request, Rev. E. Warrinner, who was pastor of the church in Huntington at
the time Nettie and her husband united there, wrote
the following :

" Some Personal Recollections of Nettie Hill Weeden.

" About the year 1874, not long after her marriage, Mrs. Weeden took up her residence in the village of Huntington, L. I., and with her husband joined by letter the Methodist Episcopal church there, of which I was pastor. Huntington was the birthplace of her father and the former home of her sainted grandmother. The church and the ministers needed helpers, and God sent us one in the person of Mrs. Weeden. It was seen at once that her soul was aglow with zeal and love for the Saviour, and as the months passed on every one was convinced that her zeal was not a flash, but an unquenchable flame.

" It was my great privilege to enjoy the aid of her prayers and sympathy and faithful labor during a large part of my ministry there. This was before she had given herself very much to evangelistic labors beyond the limits of her own church home. She was uniformly present at the services, always ready to sing, pray, or exhort, but never exhibiting vanity or ostentation, or a censorious spirit toward others who were less active than herself. She abounded in charity for the timid and silent ones, and they were often helped, and seldom or never discouraged, by her successful efforts to tell the story of the cross.

" After removing from Huntington it fell to my

lot to meet her now and then at camp-meetings, conventions, and revival services, as well as in the quiet of her own home.

"She was present at the Queens County Sunday-school Convention, in Rockville Center, in the fall of 1888. She was called out to speak on the subject of the best methods of imparting instructions to the little ones in the Sunday-school. She spoke for several minutes; then, as an illustration of one method of making truth impressive, she turned around and wrote with her finger in the air, in large capitals, a single word and sat down. She asked the audience to pronounce the word she had written, and with one voice they responded, 'Love.' I have no doubt that impressive act abides in the memory of every person present at the convention. And frequently when I walk up the aisle toward the spot where she then stood I seem to see the word 'Love' suspended in the air, though the hand that traced it is now motionless in the grave. The fact is, those letters were written not in the air merely, but on the hearts of the beholders; and her face, aglow with the radiance of Christian love, gave emphasis to the word; and, furthermore, while she illustrated a wise and simple method of instructing and impressing the little ones, she unconsciously gave us an emblem and illustration of her own Christian life.

"Her part in the drama of human life was not long

nor exceedingly conspicuous, but it was beautiful and impressive. What she did was to write in shining and golden letters the word 'LOVE' and then disappear. She wrote the word so large that there was no room on the tablet of her life for expressions of hate, envy, jealousy, or revenge.

"She came with her father and sister, Mrs. Johnson, to aid me in holding evangelistic services in Rockville Center in the spring of 1889. It was about the last of her special services in the Long Island churches. We all saw that her heart was unusually affected. She seemed to call up vividly the scenes of her father's ministry in this place many years ago, and it was interesting to watch her face while he preached and she drank in the truth as if it fell directly from the skies. Her sister, though not accustomed to accompany her in protracted meetings away from home, was permitted this time to leave her family and assist with the organ and the voice.

"For these human supports by those who were so near and dear, she seemed exceedingly thankful. She prayed, talked, and sang very sweetly. In the Sunday-school she told her experience; in the evening services she expounded, illustrated, and applied the word of God with great propriety and power. Many were deeply affected and some were happily saved.

"ROCKVILLE CENTER, L. I., *December* 26, 1889."

CHAPTER XV.

WHILE residing in Huntington she extended her labors. The call that had followed her, and was emphasized by that remarkable *dream*, or *vision*, seemed to come with stronger force. She was much exercised by it, nor could she be satisfied unless to the fullest extent of her ability she was engaged in the work she loved above all other, and to which she was evidently called.

In her "mission carriage" (for a dear friend had presented her with a beautiful horse and carriage with the understanding that "*they were to be used for the Master*") she and her husband visited on the Sabbath and week-day evenings the districts lying adjacent to her home, and attended meetings in private houses, school-houses, and churches. In these places, in song and prayer and heart exhortation, her voice was heard, and very many received her witness, and now, after the lapse of years, that voice lives in very many hearts. An instance was called up only a few days since as il-

lustrative of this. Her father on entering the church
at Huntington was accosted by a pleasant-appearing
gentleman, who cordially shook hands with him and
thus spoke : " I remember you ; at such a time you
preached in our school-house" (naming the place);
"your daughter was with you. After the sermon she
arose and spoke, and what a wonderful feeling came
over the congregation ! Every body seemed to be
moved and affected, and were in tears. Yes, I remember you ; but I shall never forget her."

Thus it was. The preacher was remembered, but
no special mention made of his sermon ; but the
daughter—that evangel—her presence and testimony
carried the hearts of all, and that voice yet lingers, as
if God continued to speak.

In July, 1882, there occurred a reunion of the " Hill
family," at Riverhead, L. I. Nettie was present, and
entered into the enjoyment of the occasion with her
usual exuberance of feeling. A large number of the
different branches of the family were there gathered.

An interesting part of that occasion, when assembled, was the address of her father, recalling up
the ancestry of the family and how death had been
busy in doing its work, and congratulating the numerous posterity represented on that occasion, and point-
ing to the meeting beyond where no ties would be
sundered or breaks occur.

Among the places visited on that occasion was the cemetery where reposed the remains of fathers, mothers, and grandparents, brothers and sisters.

To Nettie this was a most interesting place, and, as she had often done before, she knelt upon the grave of "my precious sister" and bedewed it with affection's tears, and received there a new girding for life's work and trials. Songs were sung and speeches made, and the different branches of the family separated, never all to meet again in this life. Upon **returning home** she wrote the following :

"REUNION.

" As I call the scenes before me,
    Hidden by the flight of years;
As I loose the doors of memory,
    Sweet thought my spirit cheers;
Of a home, where dwelt the sunshine,
    Of a mother's holy love,
And a father's benediction,
    Emblems of the rest above.

" Thank the Lord for this blest covering
    Thrown across the years of life;
As an angel near us hovering
    Bids us onward to the strife.
Western slopes are always sunny,
    And the days pass sweetly on,
Until they have marked the many,
    And the years of life are gone.

"Now 'tis time for their retiring,
  With the girls and boys they kneel,
And with heartfelt, true emotion,
  Pray the prayer their spirits feel:
'Lead them, O our heavenly Father,
  Through the pastures green and fair;
Let them in thy heavenly kingdom
  Each forever have a share.'

"Years have passed, that group is scattered,
  Father, mother in the church-yard lie;
Charles and William, Asa, Julia,
  Find a home beyond the sky.
But we hope again to meet them,
  When the ills of life are fled,
In that blessed, glad reunion
  Over on the other side.

"And our own sweet, gentle Anna,
  Like a flower she drooped and died;
Early crowned, she sings in glory
  Songs of Christ the Crucified.
Brighter smiles her lips are wreathing
  In that land of joy and flowers;
On the Saviour's bosom leaning,
  Roaming 'mid clestial bowers."

In looking over some old papers we came across a small pocket diary of Nettie's in which were recorded some things that occurred about this time. Called to the duties and labor of a farm home, it was quite a new life to her. It shows a little of home experience under a certain kind of pressure not common in a more public life. It is headed

" One Day's Victory.

"While residing on the farm at Huntington Harbor there came a day when I had a good deal to do; besides, I expected my dear father to visit us. So I made haste to prepare for his coming; I desired to have every thing nice and cheerful. It is surprising how unpleasant things will sometimes occur when we least expect or desire them. In sweeping I let fall on the old-fashioned hearth a parcel of nice seeds, so I stooped down and carefully gathered them up; then I thought of a certain kind of cake that pa loved, and I set about making it and put it in the oven. In a short time I looked to see if it was done. So, taking hold of the pan with my fingers, I found it too hot to hold and was obliged to drop the whole on the floor. The top of the cake, as if independent, slid off in one direction and the soft, unbaked dough in another, the whole falling in a mass at my feet. I hurriedly commenced to repair the ruin, fearing at any moment pa might come and find me in such a plight.

"Thus the forenoon passed. My husband came in at noon. I said, 'David, how have things gone on the farm to-day?' Here let me say, on this particular morning I had declared to him my need of more grace, for living on a farm was quite a different thing from going to church and being engaged in meetings all the while, and we had prayed together for extra strength, and I had gone forth feeling strong in the Lord. The mishaps I have mentioned followed in the wake of that experience.

"David replied in answer to my question, 'The lot where I have been plowing is very stony.'

"I said, 'Let us pray again; but wait a moment until I put the preserves over the fire.' So I did, and built a good fire. Then we adjourned to another room and shut the door, and made up our minds to take time to pray until victory came.

"Well, we reached that point; and I said to my husband, 'I feel strong enough to cope with a lion.' But I did not expect I should have to meet and fight smoke and burnt preserves. On opening the door the condition of things that met me I cannot fully describe.

" However, the day with its untoward events passed and evening came. In summing up the experience of the day, I had stood the test. Not a ripple had disturbed my spirit, and I hereby record it as a clear personal victory over self."

We have already related a dream that seemed to have been little less than a divine communication to Nettie. Its influence continued with her as long as she lived. It inspired her with a holy ambition to fill her " crown " with stars and to make her " robe " white and spotless.

8

Was she a dreamer? Then in her was fulfilled in these "last days" the words: "Your sons and your daughters shall prophesy, and your young men shall dream dreams." Again the Lord says, "The prophet that hath a dream, let him tell a dream." "Behold, this dreamer cometh." Among her papers we find the following:

"A Dream.

"I thought I had died; the struggle seemed past, and I realized my soul leaving the body. Before taking my flight I paused, for a short time, to view my lifeless form. There it lay in death's quiet repose. I gazed down upon the tabernacle that I had occupied since my birth. I looked upon those eyelids, now closed, from which I used to look out upon the world; those lips, from which the utterances of my life had gone forth, but were now sealed; my arms and limbs that had wrought and borne me over the rough and smooth of life. As I looked I seemed to feel a great interest in this former part of myself. I felt willing to part with it for a time, with a clear and distinct impression that I should return and again occupy the deserted house once more. I bade it an affectionate good-bye, and then took my upward flight."

In looking over this dream we see nothing unscriptural nor unreasonable. We think of the words of an inspired apostle, who said, "It is meet, as long as I am in this tabernacle, to stir you up by putting you in remembrance; knowing *that shortly I must put off this my tabernacle,* even as our Lord Jesus Christ hath showed me." Was not this to her, though in a night dream, a revelation or premonition—a fact that was to be in her future history? How vividly it came before us when, in the last sad night of her earthly existence, in obedience to the call, she did indeed "put off her tabernacle," when death's last surging wave had spent its force, and we gently closed her lips and eyes as our tears fell upon the dear form. Did not that sweet, disembodied spirit pause for a time to gaze upon the body it had left, and with feelings akin to her dream speak the affectionate farewell until again the reunion should take place?

Our dear Nettie was a firm believer in the resurrection of the body. She declared often in her public utterances that the Lord Jesus Christ would raise up *the same* body that should be laid down. She was not troubled nor distressed with " philosophical objections," so called. To her mind, taking the word of God as her guide, it did not seem to her an " incredible thing that God should raise the dead."

Some three years since she found a cocoon in the garden; it contained the apparently lifeless grub. She took it in the house and placed it by the window, where through the winter she watched it. In the spring, as the warm sun shone through the window upon the tomb of that insect, she anticipated the change. She says : " Upon getting up one morning, what was was my surprise and delight to see a large, beautiful butterfly clinging to the curtains.   There was the vacant tomb, and out from it, where for months dwelt this disgusting grub, had come forth this beautiful creature with gaudy colors, now basking in the sunlight.   Its wings were in action, rising and falling, pluming itself for its flight."   Almost in rhapsody she called us to see the wonder.   While it did not prove to her the resurrection, yet it so wonderfully illustrated and foreshadowed it to her mind as almost to carry her away with joyful anticipation in this new revelation.   To her it was a thought full of comfort. "I shall behold my dear ones again in the body."

This one question of theology was unalterably settled and fixed by the word of God.   Happy if many others who are disturbed and perplexed upon this subject would come to the same source and settle it forever in the same way.

The following are some of her musings upon the resurrection :

" THOUGHTS ON THE RESURRECTION.

" In my walks one day I found myself in a graveyard.   Passing along, my attention was drawn to a

row of old graves. Perhaps there were seven or eight.
The stones containing the inscriptions were standing
regularly at the head of each, but the mounds were
gone and the earth had sunken to a level. Save the
marble tablet there was nothing to indicate the spot
where rested the remains of those who had lived in
former years. As I stood and looked I saw the sun,
now near to setting. It shone through the fence and
cast a shadow upon those lonely graves. I thought
how true it is that sin has made for each and all a
grave; that we walk under the very shadow of death.
But just beyond is, not the setting sun, but the bright
Sun of Righteousness. This side the boundary-line
is shadow; the other, LIGHT!"

"Around the mother's knee are the children re-
peating their evening prayer. She puts the dear little ones to bed, tucks the clothes around them, and
kisses them '*good night.*' Soon the darkness passes,
then comes the morning greeting.

" So the mother lays her little ones in the grave clad
in their snowy robes. But she waits for the morning.
Morning comes, and happy celestial greetings take
place on the other side."

CHAPTER XVI.

A Young Sunday-school.—Get a Hurricane Lantern.

BEFORE leaving her Huntington home we have a few items of record made by her that we desire should appear. The following shows how intense was her desire to seize every opportunity to do something for the spiritual good of others. She writes:

"A Young Sunday-school.

"This day being the holy Sabbath I could not attend the Sabbath-school, so I sent word to the neighbors there would be one in our yard, as the weather was warm and beautiful. I had provided myself with a small blackboard, also a box of crayons, so I became artist, organist, chorister, and superintendent. Well, we had mothers, babies, and children, and all seemed pleased and I doubt not profited. I call to mind what my sainted grandmother had done sixty years before, not more than a half mile from this very spot. I feel much honored in following in her footsteps. Her work abides until this day. So our young Sunday-school was held in the orchard."

"Get a Hurricane Lantern.

"On a dark night husband and myself started from home to go to the church, distant nearly a mile. It was so dark we were obliged to light a lantern; after riding a short distance there came a gust of wind which extinguished our light.

"'Well, this is too bad; here we are in darkness; when we so much needed our light it has gone out. What shall we do?' Husband says, 'I will get a "hurricane lantern;" that kind does not blow out.' One was obtained—no danger after that; no darkness so dense but we could see; no winds so strong as to blow it out.

"There are many lights in this world, but they are uncertain. When most you need them they may go out and leave you in the dark. Must get a hurricane light. Where? Who? Jesus says, 'I am the light of the world: he that walketh in me shall not walk in darkness, but shall have the light of life.' By all means obtain the hurricane light.

"'Then let the hurricane roar.'"

CHAPTER XVII.

AFTER a few years' residence in Huntington she removed to New York. Her father at this time was pastor of Alanson Church in that city. Again into the "parsonage home," after a few years of absence, she and her husband returned. How pleasant and delightful this change was to her she most freely expressed. It did not remove her from the sphere of her chosen Christian work, but rather brought her to new and wider fields.

During her residence here she more fully consecrated herself to the Lord's service. She loved to sing, accompanied by organ or piano, Miss Frances R. Havergal's beautiful consecration hymn; and because she adopted it, making it the measure of her own consecration, we give it place in this her "memorial volume:"

> "Take my life and let it be
> Consecrated, Lord, to thee ;
> Take my hands, and let them move
> At the impulse of thy love.

"Take my feet, and let them be
Swift and beautiful for thee ;
Take my voice, and let me sing
Always, only, for my King.

"Take my lips, and let them be
Filled with messages for thee ;
Take my moments, and my days,
Let them flow in ceaseless praise.

"Take my will and make it thine,
It shall be no longer mine ;
Take my heart, it is thine own,
It shall be thy royal throne.

"Take my love; my Lord, I pour
At thy feet its treasure store ;
Take myself, and I will be
Ever, only, all for thee."

In looking over her subsequent life, and taking carefully its measure, we conclude that all that hymn expressed found a beautiful illustration in her experience. She was emphatic in declaiming the word "all," and to her it meant all and FOREVER!

In her public labors many warm and pressing invitations were received by her from both pastors and people, to which she responded. The form of her services would vary; sometimes it would be a Bible-reading, then she would select a single passage of Scripture and make that the basis of her remarks; sometimes her exercises would consist in part of a "song service," which she would lead herself on organ or piano, modestly occupying a place in the altar in preference to the pulpit. Although often taking a single text, she would never consent to call it preaching. "I am not a preacher," she would say; "I talk to the people and tell them of Jesus and his salvation."

Among her papers are many fragments and sketches, partly written, with allusions to scenes of which she herself had been an eye-witness, of illustration and anecdote. To read them they are incomplete; they needed the inspiration of her heart, voice, and eyes to bring them forth clothed with freshness and feeling— *prophetic utterances* that often would startle the sleeping conscience, or by magnetic touch bless the hearts of God's dear children. We insert from her papers the following:

"'And now, Little Children, Abide in Him.'
(1 John 2. 28.)

"This book is full of good things inspired of God. Their voice is not for one age or part of the world, but for all time and every land. To *us* and to all nations is the word of this salvation sent. Paul—good, holy Paul—writes with the crown of martyrdom in view, 'I am ready to be offered, and the time of my departure is at hand; henceforth there is laid up for

me a crown.' David, the 'sweet singer,' though centuries have rolled away, sings on to-day, 'The Lord is
my shepherd, I shall not want.' The evangelical
prophet in golden language told of His coming on
whose 'shoulders the government was to be laid.' The
same becomes to us to-day the 'mighty God, the
everlasting Father, the Prince of Peace.'

"John, the beloved disciple, having caught the spirit
of his Master when a young man, now old and bending under the weight of years, speaks down through
the ages to us to-day, 'And now, little children, abide
in him.' It would appear as if he had a pre-emptive
right to this endearing term 'little children,' as he so
frequently uses it. It is full of love and gentleness.

"Naturally such was not his nature, for we learn
himself and brother were called 'sons of thunder,'
and at one time asked permission of the Saviour to
'call down fire from heaven' upon certain ones because they followed not after them, which spirit was
rebuked by the Master. But ever after Pentecost the
loving spirit of his Saviour dominated all his being—
no more fire to consume and destroy, no narrow prej-
udice that could see no good only as it appeared in
their way. Companionship with Jesus changed the
entire current of his being; even his words are such
as Jesus used, 'Little children, abide in him.'

"We cannot literally walk with him as did the disciples, but we can study his life; this will wonderfully shape our thoughts and turn them into the same current.

" Recently I attended a meeting in which the leader requested those who gave testimony to take from the life of Jesus that which had most impressed them. A minister's wife arose and said: ' These words, " And he must needs go through Samaria," have been running through my mind. Upon looking to find the reason I discovered why—it was to meet and bless a poor outcast woman.' Another lady arose and said that ' Jesus in the house at Bethany has very deeply moved my heart, because there he had spoken words of comfort to the two bereaved sisters about their dead brother;' and while she thus spoke burst into a flood of tears, for she, too, had recently lost a dear brother. Still another, lately saved, ' was happy to think that Jesus opened the eyes of the blind, thus giving them sight; and he has touched my blind eyes, and now I see.' And another arose and sang in subdued tones:

> " ' Calvary, dark Calvary,
> Where Jesus gave his life for me ;
> 'Twas there my sorrow died.'

" Thus as we look at the wonderful Jesus and his words, ' We are changed from glory to glory as by the Spirit of the Lord.'

"To '*abide in him.*' I became so interested in this word 'abide,' that I desired to get all its meaning. So I took my dictionary and found its signification was broadened as I read its definition: '*To rest,* or *dwell; to remain,* or *continue.*' So, then, it came to me as a place of rest, and in this rest there was —safety.

"On the frontier life of our country, when Indians prowled around to destroy the lives of the early settlers, it became necessary to have a place of refuge; so they built a 'block-house.' Thither upon the first signal of alarm they were to fly, and when once they had reached it and the door was closed they were safe. It is even so in this world where spiritual foes lurk around to hunt our lives and to destroy us. But Jesus becomes to us a pavilion of shelter and safety. Paul said to his shipwrecked companions, 'Except ye *abide* in the ship ye cannot be saved.' To us Jesus is the only place of safety. But to abide in Jesus means A HAPPY LIFE. When Jesus walked among men he saw the world in a state of disquiet and unrest. He spoke words of heart's-ease when he said, 'Come unto me, all ye that labor and are heavy laden, and I will give you rest;' words that throw joy and sunshine into the soul, and bring 'rest' by becoming our burden-bearer. 'Take my yoke upon you, and learn of me; for my yoke is easy and my burden is light.' Let us learn, dear ones, how to give our burdens to Jesus. He bore our sins, so will he carry our burdens.

"'Here bring your wounded hearts, here tell your anguish;
Earth has no sorrow that heaven cannot heal.'

But more, for us it means A SINLESS LIFE.

"To prove this I do not take you to human creeds, but to God's word: 'Whosoever *abideth* in him sinneth not.' 'Whosoever is born of God doth not commit sin.' 'He that committeth sin is of the devil.' 'For this purpose was the Son of God manifested, that he might destroy the works of the devil.'

"In the presence of these Scriptures there need be no controversy, no misgivings. Our blessed Jesus not only saves from sin, but keeps us from sinning. Do some say 'Impossible?' I answer, 'His name shall be called Jesus, for he shall save his people from their sins.' But abiding in Christ means SUCCESS IN CHRISTIAN LABOR. This is what we much desire to know— how we may reach success in our work. With all the plans and appliances used there is but one royal road to success; we have it here. 'Abide in me, and I in you. As the branch cannot bear fruit of itself, except it abide in the vine; no more can ye, except ye abide in me.' 'He that abideth in me, and I in him, the same bringeth forth much fruit.' Coupled with fruit-bearing comes also the TRUE SECRET OF PREVAILING

PRAYER. 'If ye abide in me, and my words abide in you, ye shall ask what ye will, and it shall be done unto you.' Wonderful words ! Without limit, only circumscribed by our needs and Christ's omnipotence. You remember how a poor woman came to Christ with a heart breaking with sorrow, for her dear child was being tortured by the devil; how for a time Jesus repulsed her ; but agony and faith conquered when he said, ' O woman, great is thy faith ; *be it unto thee as thou wilt.*' As much as if he had said, ' Go, have it all your own way.'

"Dear Christian ones in this world of sorrow, it is ours to be happy. This comes of ' Christ abiding.' ' The joy of the Lord is your strength.' ' Rejoice in the Lord always.' ' Christ in you the hope of glory.' How it smoothes the roughness of this life, and claims all the promises for the life to come. ' I go to prepare a place for you. And if I go and prepare a place for you, I will come again, and receive you unto myself ; that where I am, there ye may be also."

> " ' He is fitting up a mansion
> Which eternally shall stand.'

"Some years ago a dear friend built a home for himself when he should retire from the activities of life. The children were young, some of them small. In the plan of the house a room was planned for father and mother, another for the daughters, and one for the son. After a time the house was finished ; the parents came to reside in this newly completed home ; but where are the daughters ? They have grown to woman's estate, and have now homes of their own. Where is the little boy who was to occupy the pleasant room, arranged and planned for him ? Now he is a man ; business calls him away. Father and mother are there, but they are alone ; the dear children are gone. Occasionally they visit the home, and when about leaving mother follows them to the gate, and there is something that sounds very much like a sigh, and she hurriedly brushes away the fallen tear as the good-bye is spoken ; and as she returns she declares it is 'lonesome without the children.' The home is there, the house is neatly furnished, but where are the girls and boy ? And when the autumn passes, and the winds get chilly, the key is turned on the home, and the 'precious ones' sit by the fireside of their children at their homes.

" So the blessed Saviour is preparing a home for each and all; a mansion for Mary and John, for father and mother, and Jesus will be there, and all the family, for they are blood-washed. ' That where I am, there ye may be also.' O, what a 'gathering that will be.' O, this abiding ! It is reciprocal, the two parties agree. 'I in them, and thou in me.' No emergency can arise that cannot be met by this precious indwelling Saviour. Always at home, always ready. Earthly friendships sometimes fail; the pleasant smile of to-day often gives place to the frown of to-morrow; the welcome of the morning is shadowed by the cloud of the evening. Not so to him who abides in Christ, who summers and winters with him. He will turn the crust of a scanty meal into a royal feast, and he himself will partake of that feast with us. Our homes will be remodeled, because our divine Guest has come to abide and stay. Pictures of evil imagination, worldliness, and pride that hung around are taken down, and pure and holy ones adorn the walls of this soul home. The old furniture, that represented selfishness and temper, is removed and sent away, and hope, love, and faith take their place.

" Recently in a large boarding-house, where people had come to enjoy the summer months, in the midst of their pleasure they heard that one of the guests had been seized with a severe illness. It was feared it might be contagious. Very quickly trunks were packed, and in a short time the rooms of that house were silent and empty. Not so with our abiding Christ. He has come to stay. No disease or casualty can frighten him away. He, in the days of his flesh, did not fear the leper's touch, so now he will kiss the fevered brow and lip, for

9

> " 'The healing of the seamless dress
> Is by our beds of pain ;
> We touch him in life's throng and press,
> And we are whole again.'

No caste, condition, or color can change his heart or keep him away.

"Near my residence there was a little colored boy about ten years of age sick of consumption. His mother was very poor, so she was obliged to leave him with the other children while she went out to work. One day he seems to be worse, and with moaning voice asks to be carried up stairs. After awhile the sister is ready, and now, says the little tired boy, ' Hold me a little while and sing before you take me up ; ' and the noisy children stop their play. The sister asks, ' What shall we sing?' and he feebly answers :

> " 'On Jordan's stormy banks I stand,
> And cast a wishful eye
> To Canaan's fair and happy land,
> Where my possessions lie.'

The noisy group listen or sing. 'Now take me up stairs and lay me on my bed.' She does so. In a short time the sister goes to the bed again ; his eyes are closed, his hands are folded, and he is gone. He had heard his sister sing, but sweeter music had struck his ear from angel voice ; he had crossed the swellings of Jordan and gone to dwell with Jesus.

" 'We do all fade as the leaf.' An inevitable law writes *change* on every thing. In our home there is a little box containing treasures. From it we take a ringlet of golden hue; it scarcely seems as if this could have been taken from the brow of that one

> " ' Where now in quiet grace
> The locks of gray are resting.'

Our homes, the Eden-spots of life, are changing. There is a little 'high-chair' carefully put away. What does it mean? Out of sight in a drawer is a pair of little shoes half worn. Occasionally they are taken out, wet with tears, and silently returned.

" Well do I call to mind when moving-time came in our home; a certain little chest was emptied, and dresses and bonnets and shoes of a little four-year-old girl would be hung out for a while, then kissed and put away again. In the corner of the room there stands grandfather's cane. He will never need it again, for he has gone where they are never old. In the parlor, amid the furniture of modern style, there is a basket; it is old-fashioned, it seems out of place. You ask, ' What is this?' The answer comes, ' That was grandmother's work-basket.' But she has gone to join grandfather on the other shore. These are only precious relics that link us with the past. But, O, how the heart mourns as we remember them!

How delightful to call to mind just here that in Jesus we have a changeless, undying friend. In sorrow the same, in youth and old age the same. Thus sang the immortal poet of Methodism:

> " 'In age and feebleness extreme,
> Who shall a helpless worm redeem ?
> Jesus, my only hope thou art;
> Strength of my failing flesh and heart;
> O, could I catch one smile from thee
> And drop into eternity!'

> " 'Abide with me! Fast falls the eventide,
> The darkness deepens—Lord, with me abide!
> When other helpers fail, and comforts flee,
> Help of the helpless, *O abide with me!*

> " 'Hold thou thy cross before my closing eyes;
> Shine through the gloom and point me to the skies;
> Heaven's morning breaks, and earth's vain shadows flee;
> In life, in death, O Lord, *abide with me!*' "

These extracts are only fragmentary. They show, however, the leading of her mind. If to these were added her personal presence, with a rich, melodious voice, an eye supernaturally illuminated, and every expression of her countenance almost transfigured, we should get the full idea of the discourse about her " Abiding Saviour."

CHAPTER XVIII.

HOME LIFE.—BIRTHDAY GREETINGS.—FATHER.—MOTHER.—HUSBAND.—
R. RHOADES, THE OLD FRIEND, AGED EIGHTY YEARS.—A FRIEND,
JOHN B. HOPKINS.

WE have spoken much of her home life. It was here especially her queenly, magnetic presence was felt. To scatter sunshine and happiness over that circle was her greatest delight. Every occasion or passing event that could be used was seized upon and laid under contribution to that end.

Scattered through the year were the birthdays of the "dear ones at home." These were not allowed to pass without being observed. At the home and table of father and mother, or her own, all the members of the household would gather. Not much of a feast would be prepared, but a large and beautiful cake, usually prepared by her own hand, would grace the center of the table. Upon it, in large iced letters, would appear the name and age of the one whose birthday was to be celebrated. Lying under the plate some verses were placed, after which Mr. Wesley's grace was spoken by all.

"Be present at this our table, Lord;
Be here, as every-where, adored;
Thy creatures bless, and grant that we
May feast in paradise with thee."

The verses were read by the birthday member, and the joy of the hour would be complete.

As our dear Nettie was the central mover of these occasions we may be pardoned from bringing out from that home circle what otherwise would hardly be admissible. These were parts of her interesting life that made her so dear to us all. By fitness and unanimous consent she was president and secretary of that "home club," and always gave notice of those occasions as well as contributed to carry them through.

Here we introduce a few of the many. As the anniversary days came and passed each one was observed and stood up along the highway as so many milestones of human life :

"FATHER.—BIRTHDAY GREETING.

" Welcome, dear father, to the day
To which we now have come!
We would with flowers strew your way
As you come to — 61.

" Of all the golden threads of life
That all the years have spun,
This is the brightest in the woof,
The joyous — 61.

"Youth had its springtime and its flowers,
    Its pleasures and its fun,
But still more beautiful the hours
    That circle — 61."

"To my Mother.—Greeting.

" Full sixty years ago to-day
    Since you the threshold crossed,
Since you began your pilgrim way,
    And on life's billows tossed.

" Sixty years, how long it seems,
    As we look back to-day;
And yet how very like a dream
    Or vision of the day.

" The woven chain of sixty years
    Links memory with the past;
And other forms than these to-day
    Are with us in our feast.

" The mother fond, that o'er you bent
    With tenderness and love,
And praised the gift that God had sent,
    Long since has gone above.

" The one you chose of all the rest
    To walk life's rugged way,
With sixty years has, too, been blessed,
    And by you sits to-day.

" The little household group are here,
    Save one, before us gone
To view the better world so fair,
    And stands before the throne.

" Our darling Anna now has gone
　　To join the ranks above;
But we will say, 'God's will be done;'
　　He did it all in love.

" And so the three that are left behind
　　Greet you with joyous lay,
And ne'er will richer treasure find
　　Than mother's love to-day."

" To my Dear Husband.—Greeting.

" Now upon this joyous hour
　　Hear the warble of your mate,
As beneath this pleasant bower
　　You to-day are — 48.

" Out upon life's restless river
　　You are borne at rapid rate;
Not a moment can you linger
　　As you signal — 48.

" Gray and white your beard is growing,
　　Bald and shining is your pate;
This is altogether owing
　　To your being — 48.

" Saviour, bless my own dear Weedie
　　As he nears to heaven's gate;
Give him grace and give him glory
　　As he passes — 48."

In the family and home of Mr. Richard Rhoades,
Sr., in Jamaica, Nettie and her husband first took up
their abode after their marriage. A very pleasant

home it was to her, and ever after she entertained for those dear friends a warm and loving remembrance. A number of deeply interesting occasions took place in the family in which Nettie participated. Only two may be mentioned. This item appeared in the village paper :

" A Birthday Celebration.

" On Tuesday evening last a number of friends of Mr. Richard Rhoades, of Union Avenue, called and congratulated him on his eightieth birthday. A pleasing feature of the occasion was the reading of a beautiful and appropriate poem on the event composed by Mrs. Nettie Hill Weeden.

" ' To Brother Rhoades on His Eightieth Birthday.

" ' Our happy greeting, brother, friend,
    We give to you this day,
While in your home an hour we spend
    To cheer you on your way.

" ' Full eighty years in life's long strife
    You have your burdens borne;
The joys and sorrows of this life
    Have filled your earthly song.

" ' List! we will walk through memory's halls,
    Talk gently with the past;
While on our ear sweet voices fall
    That we have loved the best.

" ' A mother dear her precious boy *
　　Now folds within her arms,
Where naught of strife can e'er alloy,
　　Or wake to rude alarms.

" ' That mother fond, who loved so well,
　　Has passed the shores of time;
Has now gone home with Christ to dwell
　　In that fair, sunny clime.

" ' The father's gone, his race was run
　　Full many years ago;
And other friends, their journeys done,
　　Have finished all below.

" ' Another gentle form draws near,†
　　In spotless garments dressed,
And says, in accents soft and clear,
　　" I dwell among the blessed."

" ' And so the friends of early youth
　　And riper years are gone;
But He who is the Life, the Truth,
　　Yet bids you travel on.

" ' For God has spared your only boy,
　　An " Isaac " in your age,
To be a comfort and a joy
　　Along life's pilgrimage.

" ' Nor fear the darkness of the way,
　　He is there the light;
You're traveling on to endless day,
　　A land where all is bright.

---

* His mother, aged nearly a hundred years, had recently died.
† His dear and excellent wife, also, had just departed to be with Christ.

" ' No darksome clouds can there arise
  Above the crystal sea;
The bow of promise spans the skies
  And earthly shadows flee.

" ' The best of all is yet to come—
  The joy and rest of heaven,
The pleasures of the mansion home
  To all who are forgiven.

" ' May He who kept thee eighty years
  Be still thy hope and stay,
Till in the land that knows no tears
  You'll dwell in cloudless day.

" *January* 11, 1887.   NETTIE.' "

The following birthday-greeting was written by
Nettie and read on the occasion, accompanied by a
beautiful presentation. This half-century celebration
was one of much interest and none enjoyed it more
than she:

" To BROTHER JOHN B. HOPKINS ON HIS FIFTIETH BIRTHDAY.

—GREETING.

  " We now meet again together,
    On this joyous, festive night,
  To exchange with one another
    Thoughts and happy greetings bright.
  Heaven bless thee on thy journey,
    Strew thy path with blessings rare,
  Ever lead and ever keep thee
    Free from sorrow, want, and care.

" *Fifty years* upon life's journey,
   Sailing for the blessed port ;
Peaceful still, or wild commotion,
   What for you these years have wrought.
Let us touch the door of mem'ry
   With the mystic wand of love,
Give ourselves awhile to reverie,
   As from scene to scene we rove.

" Home again—a child with mother;
   In her arms she folds her boy,
Loves and tends him as none other,
   You are still her pride and joy.
Father, too, looks on you fondly,
   Prays that heaven may bless his son ;
It's the prayer that's offered only
   For the young and tender one.

" Childhood's gone; its hours—how fleeting;
   'Mid youth's bowers now you play;
Merry sunsets, happy greetings,
   Life seems but a summer's day.
Pass you on to scenes of folly,
   When to other years you come ;
But you heard the ' Old, old story:'
   Praise the Lord, the lost is found.

"Found for Jesus, found for heaven,
   Found his precious love to tell ;
Love that, all your sins forgiven,
   Asks you ever with him to dwell.
So you told the wondrous story,
   Bid the trembling sinner come
To the Lord of life and glory,
   And in him to find a home.

"Then you took your market-wagon,
  And the loving ones you sought ;
Fearing not, though heavy laden,
  For they *must* to Christ be brought.
And like Philip, in the Scriptures,
  You would have them 'come and see.'
Yes, they came, and, O, what rapture,
  As they sing—Salvation's free.

"Thus the seed on life's broad river
  Scattered. It will come again,
Looking only to the Giver
  Of the sunshine and the rain.
Now, already some are gathered
  In the happy harvest home ;
From the storms of life are sheltered,
  And rejoice before the throne.

"Time has passed thus swiftly o'er thee,
  Moments, days, and years are fled ;
Some that started on the journey
  Now are numbered with the dead.
Father's gone, no more he meets thee
  Here upon the shores of time,
But awaits with joy to greet thee
  In that blessed sunny clime.

"*Fifty years*, and now you gather
  Sons and daughters by your side;
With the loving wife and mother
  In this happy home reside.
With a form and heart so noble,
  God has added to your store,
Not alone of gold or silver,
  But the blessings of the poor.

"Swifter than the weaver's shuttle,
  As it passes to and fro,
You are pressing through life's battle,
  Ever conquering as you go.
Always close to your Commander,
  Keep the precious armor bright ;
Never to the foe surrender,
  'Till you're *victor* in the fight.

" Nettie Hill Weeden.

"*April* 1, 1887."

CHAPTER XIX.

Camp-meetings.—Merrick, L. I.—Charge of Young People's and Children's Meeting.—Presiding Elder Rev. B. M. Adams's Letter.—Thomas Lucky.—Tabernacle.—Love for Children.—Wilt Thou be Made Whole?—Poem.

CAMP-MEETINGS have been a distinct form of religious service, and very closely identified with Methodism on Long Island. In the churches their usefulness and influence have been recognized. In Nettie's life and experience she was early brought into contact with these special religious gatherings. When a child she was taken by her parents, and she continued to attend them as long as she lived. No place seemed to her more sweet and sacred than these convocations of God's dear people in groves or wood. To her they were occasions of much spiritual enjoyment; they also afforded her opportunities of Christian work which she ever improved.

With the Merrick meeting on Long Island especially did she not only become deeply interested from its first organization, but closely identified with its history and work. For a number of years she was called to take charge of that interesting department—the youth's and children's meetings.

The following letter of invitation from the Rev. B. M. Adams, presiding-elder of the district, will show the high esteem in which her services were held. This invitation received and responded to will be read with unusual interest. It was her last meeting at Merrick, and occurred but a few weeks before there came the heavenly call, "Come up higher," when she passed to the great encampment with Jesus and glorified saints before the throne.

This meeting was to her one of much enjoyment. Many friends who saw her work and listened to her words and song declare it to have been the most beautiful and impressive of her life. How many children and young people will date their awakening and conversion at this meeting and former ones led by her it is impossible to tell. We firmly believe a goodly number brought to Jesus at the Merrick campground will in that day become a beautiful setting in her crown to shine as "stars for ever and ever." Here follows the letter:

"203 PROSPECT PLACE, BROOKLYN, }
"June 5, 1888. }

"DEAR SISTER WEEDEN: The children's department at Merrick Camp-meeting has been so long under your successful management that we should deem it a cold day when you could not be with us; and so it gives me great pleasure to invite you to take charge again this year. I am *daily* praying now for the work. In accordance with a covenant made last year I have prayed every Sunday morning, but of late have taken to asking the Lord every day for the meeting and the workers. Of course, you came in for a share. What wonders of power we might see there if——. You are aware, perhaps, that the meeting this year is July 17 to 27. The change has been made for several reasons: the ministers are not away on their vacations; the summer boarder has not yet come out in the swarming of August; the weather may be assumed to be warm at that time; the presiding elder can be there (I go to Chautauqua again this year, August 6). Have you read the new act of the General Conference relating to deaconnesses? Do you know, I thought of you the first second I read the act. The thing cannot go into effect immediately, but some good women I know of are going to be wanted before long. I am burdened for my district, and am crying to the Lord for his mighty help, that salvation may come to us. Please write me your acceptance of the invitation. With regards to your husband,

" Yours,   B. M. Adams."

As she was so closely related to the place and that department of the work for a number of years, we

10

are permitted to produce the beautiful cut belonging to the Camp-meeting Association, to which we have added her presence. She is seen directly in front of the platform and pulpit, with her sister presiding at the organ. Here daily she held her young people's and children's meeting, and so deeply interested were they that in addition large numbers would gather to hear from her the sweet story of the cross so simple and yet so impressive.

To assist her in her work she used the blackboard, thus addressing the heart through the eye as well as the ear. She usually did the sketching herself, bringing therefrom illustrations at once so simple and attractive as to arrest and hold the closest attention of her audiences. Her music on the organ, acccompanied by her voice, would lead out the songs of the young until the grove would be almost filled with celestial melodies. She possessed a remarkable power over childhood, so that large numbers were won to her heart and teachings. What the secret was that gave her this power we may see in part.

First, *she loved children.* She did not have to cultivate that affection, it was natural; so that in her intercourse with them they quickly saw and felt it. She possessed the faculty of presenting the truth in a pleasant, winning way, so simple and plain that the feeblest mind could understand. Her fund of

SETTLE CONDUCTING THE YOUNG PEOPLE'S MEETING AT MERRICK CAMP-MEETING, LONG ISLAND.

anecdote and illustration was large and appropriately selected ; nothing coarse or rough would be allowed ; the very best and purest only could be used by her in this work; and it cost her no little thought and labor to gather the material to be used, which when employed was followed by much anxiety lest after all it should fail. Hence her devout and earnest prayers in secret and in public places, that the Lord would use her honest and sincere endeavors in the conversion of the youth and children. She believed that in childhood they should be brought to the Saviour. Upon this subject there is not a little skepticism in the Church ; but it was never shared by her. She was always anxious until this result was reached. She saw, also, and felt the great importance of the Holy Spirit in this work. She knew enough of the depravity of the human heart, its perverseness, and the stubbornness of the will not to expect success unless the divine Spirit should work and subdue. Hence she always sought for the presence and help of the Spirit. She believed and often declared her " faith in the conversion of children "—that they were as genuine and lasting as those brought to Christ in later years.

The following lines I find among her papers ; they illustrate her faith in childhood conversion as well as the longing of her soul for the same :

"WILT THOU BE MADE WHOLE?

"Will you come and seek the Saviour?
    Will you seek him in your youth?
Will you come and find him precious,
    He the life, the way, the truth?

"Will you leave your life of folly?
    Lay your sins and sorrows down?
Come and walk a way most holy,
    Which leads to a blessed crown?

"At the cross you first must linger,
    Where the blessed Jesus died;
Be no longer now a stranger
    To the Saviour crucified.

"Claim the precious Holy Spirit,
    As he hovers round thy soul;
O, the gift of peace inherit,
    Christ the Saviour makes thee whole.

"If you are with sorrow laden,
    Cast it all at Jesus' feet;
He will make your soul a heaven,
    Filled with love and joy complete.

"Are you clinging to some idol
    Hid away within your heart?
Take the blessed holy Bible,
    And from every idol part.

"Do you fear the laugh and jeering
    Of a lost and ruined soul?
Come to Jesus, nothing fearing,
    Christ thy Saviour makes thee whole."

CHAPTER XX.

Return to Jamaica.—Religious Life Expanded.—Temperance Work.
—W. C. T. U.—Resolutions From the Same.—Extracts From
Diary.—Lawrence, L. I.—Faint, Yet Pursuing.—Matthew 27. 1.

AFTER an absence of a few years Nettie returned again to Jamaica, where she remained in sweet fellowship with the Church and devoted a considerable portion of her time in evangelistic labors until the summons came to a higher and nobler work before the throne.

During these few last years her religious life and experience wonderfully expanded, while her field of operation in Christian work became very much enlarged. As she stepped out, with stronger faith, with a love that became almost a consuming passion, with a singular distrust in herself, she chose Paul's words for her motto: "I can do all things through Christ strengthening me." She went forth, and much success crowned her labors.

About this time her mind was turned very much toward the temperance work. Heretofore she had felt how great was the curse of strong drink, and she had lifted up her voice against it; but it remained for these few last years to intensify and burn the idea into her soul. She now saw it to be her duty to give more time and sacrifice to this work; hence, in public and private she lifted up her voice against the awful scourge.

In the village where she resided there was a noble band of Christian women belonging to the Woman's Christian Temperance Union. With these she joined herself and commenced to do battle against this worst foe of humanity. There was a fruitful field just at home. A center of work was started in Beaver Street, where aggressive operations were put forth. Here Nettie labored. While the majority of those among whom she wrought were young, yet there were older ones brought within the reach of these Christian workers. Here she talked and sang; using the organ to assist her in her work, and a blackboard to illustrate. Thus this truly missionary work went on, and it is not too much to say that hopeful results were realized. Very many of those who heard her voice and saw her work will carry her in their memories as long as they live.

To exhibit her love and interest in this work we here present a letter written to those who were co-workers with her:

"JAMAICA, October 5, 1888.

"DEAR SISTERS OF THE W. C. T. U.: Lest you might think strange of my continued absence from your meetings, also those held in Beaver Street, I thought it well to write you. Engagements attendant upon other parts of the great work, to which I gave myself years ago, have prevented my being with you.

" I am growing in my enthusiasm and love for the temperance work. Never before have I found such opportunities for labor in this cause as now. I find it really a part of the work in which I am engaged. I see a great demand for more laborers. As we go forward it multiplies on our hands.

" As to the meetings held in Beaver Street, I hope they will be continued; but they should be so on a strictly religious basis. In this direction only can they be controlled so as to have character and success. By observing this should numbers fall away, yet there will be a better foundation for success a little farther on. I have conversed with some good workers in the cause, and they come to the same conclusion. There is needed something beneath and behind the pledge to give it force and permanency. It needs Christianity to come in to make the work royally successful.

" I desire to bring before the ' Union ' a suggestion about a blackboard. Those who have attended our meetings have seen how difficult it is to gain and keep the attention of many of those who compose our gatherings. Would not illustrations on a blackboard work well? I brought the matter before the meeting two evenings, and it was almost a surprise to me how freely they responded with contributions enough to purchase one. I told them the ladies would get it mounted for them. I did this mostly upon my own responsibility, as I had not time to confer with you about it. When the board was purchased and put in the rooms I did not think I should be absent so much.

"Now, will the ladies of the 'Union' take the work I would gladly perform myself? See that it is put in a proper place, and that some one draws something upon it that will interest and instruct those who attend. Who will help in this little plan, so as to benefit those that attend our meetings? I shall gladly be present whenever it is possible. Praying that the blessing of prosperity and success may attend the good work,

"Yours in Christian fellowship,

"NETTIE HILL WEEDEN."

The following, written to the Secretary of the W. C. T. U., will explain itself:

"MRS. CRANE.

"DEAR SISTER: Inclosed you will find a letter. Will you please read it at your next meeting held in Beaver Street? After what occurred at our last gathering there an explanation in regard to my absence seems to be necessary. Never has my way so fully opened to go out to labor in the vineyard as now. 'The harvest truly is great, but the laborers are few.' Pray for me, that while I go in weakness I may fully trust in the strength of Jesus, so I may at the close of my day return, bringing golden sheaves with me not a few.

"P. S.—Would be glad to receive a letter from you about our meetings at any time during the coming month, sent to Huntington, as my work will be for a time in that direction."

"JAMAICA, October 3, 1888.

"TO THE BOYS AND GIRLS, MEN AND WOMEN OF THE BEAVER STREET TEMPERANCE MEETING:

"You cannot tell how gladly I would be with you, but my absence prevents. I have written to the ladies to get the blackboard mounted and set in the room, also to get some one to draw on the board until I return home, when I shall do it myself.

"I hope you will attend the meetings, and be very quiet, that you may hear what the good ladies have to say to you, and learn to be very good yourselves, asking Jesus to help you.

"Your dear friend,
"MRS. NETTIE HILL WEEDEN."

In this work and with that truly excellent band of Christian laborers Nettie was greatly delighted, and in the coming months she anticipated much pleasure and success. But in this she was not permitted. Out from this band of loving workers she was removed to higher and more advanced work in another part of God's realm.

How great the loss to her sister co-workers we get from the following resolutions forwarded to her afflicted and bereaved husband:

"At a meeting of the Jamaica Woman's Christian Temperance Union held on Friday, October 4, 1889, the following resolutions were unanimously adopted:

"WHEREAS, God in his providence has suddenly removed from among us our beloved sister, Mrs. Nettie Hill Weeden, therefore be it

"*Resolved*, That in the death of Mrs. Weeden this Union loses one of its most earnest and devoted members—a woman whose life was consecrated to the service of the Master; like him she 'went about doing good.'

"*Resolved*, That her lovely and useful Christian life shall be held in affectionate remembrance by us all, helping us to work more zealously while the day lasts. 'She being dead, yet speaketh.'

"*Resolved*, That a copy of these resolutions be sent

to the family of Mrs. Weeden, and also printed in the village papers.

"Mrs. C. H. Harris, *President.*

"M. L. McCormick, *Secretary.*"

In the following pages we give a few brief extracts furnished from her diary. When written it is doubtful if she ever expected they would be made public. They introduce to us the manner and spirit of her labor. They show to us, also, how ardently she longed for the conversion of sinners, as well as the sanctification of believers.

"December 11, 1885.—Came to Lawrence by invitation from the pastor, Rev. William Ross. My husband and I went to the church on Saturday evening. On Sunday morning Brother Ross invited us to "go forward" as the Lord should lead us. I spoke a short time in regard to the unfaithfulness of the past—how many there were who had done but little during the year now nearly gone. I asked all those who desired to receive the blessed fullness, and thus become fitted for work, to come forward and kneel with myself at the altar. Quite a number came. I sang, inviting others to join me in the old song, 'Refining fire, go through my heart.' While thus kneeling I spoke of refining fire, of sanctifying power, after which I definitely gave my testimony as to how

I sought it, how sorely I was tempted in regard to the term, and how God gave me the victory; then specially invited all who truly desired it, and would pray for it as a distinct blessing, to come forward and thus be known as seekers for heart-purity. Quite a number responded to the call. It was a time of deep interest, and some 'entered' into the blessed rest of faith.

" The first meeting closed with victory on the Lord's side. In the afternoon a storm set in. O that the Lord would visit the people at their homes! In the evening the church was unopened by reason of the storm. We, however, went to the parsonage, where we held a prayer-meeting. I read Christ's Sermon on the Mount.

" God met us there. After singing a song of praise we returned home. Thus ends the first Sabbath at Lawrence.

> " ' My faith looks up to thee,
> Thou Lamb of Calvary,
> Saviour divine.' "

" Monday evening, December 13.—Through the storm we again went to Lawrence. This evening the church was opened and lighted. Not many present. I referred to the resolutions of the Sabbath, and again desired those who had power to work, or strength to live, as true witnesses for the Master to join me at the altar. Some of the brethren came. I moved out in the congregation and spoke to an unconverted man.

He seemed to feel his need of a Saviour. I urged him to go to Jesus. I trust the Spirit will draw him. I then spoke from our Lord's words: 'He that believeth shall be saved; and he that believeth not shall be damned.' I told of a man who in despair went about crying, 'Lost! lost! lost!' and of a young man who, in a dream, thought he was being turned away upon the left hand, saw his devoted mother, and, crying out, 'O, mother, mother, save me!' he awoke and gave his heart to God. I earnestly entreated the church to pray for souls. So ends another meeting. God grant that good results may be realized!"

"December 15.—Evening finds us again in the house of God. I sang the old hymn, 'Alas! and did my Saviour bleed?' Brother Ross, the pastor, then spoke and prayed, after which I stood up in the Lord's name and declared from Matt. 27. 1: 'Cruel words! Judas had delivered Christ to the multitude, but under remorse returns the price and casts it down in the presence of the elders and chief priests, saying, "I have sinned in that I have betrayed innocent blood."'

"'Conscience-money—the "price of blood." Judas could not keep it. The chief priests would not take it. Many sell Christ in their business transactions for a little gain—sell their influence, barter away their Christian joy; but when they get the price, like Judas, don't know what to do with it. Is it a field gained?

The curse is upon it. Whatever it may be, if gained unlawfully it will prove a field of blood. How many have brought "conscience-money!" How often is God's work hindered by some cause unknown to others. O God, help us to get right! Jesus stands before the governor. How often the poor sinner invites God's judgments. I heard of a young man returning from church who asked one of his comrades how far it was to hell; in a few moments he was thrown from his horse and killed. Inviting God's judgments by neglecting mercy. Pilate washes his hands in token of innocency, but soon scourges Jesus. Inconstancy! How many acknowledge him to-day and deny him to-morrow! Question: "What shall we do with Jesus?" Some, as in olden times, cry, "Crucify him!" The question to you awaits an answer. Now they take him to the common hall, where they strip him and put on the scarlet robe and crown of thorns, and mockingly bow before him.'

"I then tenderly endeavored to depict the scene of the crucifixion; I desired them to look to Calvary.

> "'See, from his head, his hands, his feet,
> Sorrow and love flow mingled down:
> Did e'er such love and sorrow meet,
> Or thorns compose so rich a crown?'

I urged the church and sinners to make a grand rally around the cross. I pressed the question, What is the best time to seek the Lord? How large the proportion of those who seek the Lord do so in their youth! The sure promise is to the early seeker. A number of testimonies followed, in which confession was made unto salvation. Thus ends another meeting. 'I praise the Lord for his goodness.' "

This diary runs along through successive nights, wherein we see how greatly the heart of this now sainted woman was drawn out toward God and in behalf of souls. And yet something hindered; the blessing seemed to delay.

" On one of the following nights Brother Ross arose and said, ' What more can we do? ' I replied, ' Keep on smiting the rock, and don't be discouraged if there are no visible results. We will do it for Jesus's sake.' After singing ' The Lily of the Valley ' the meeting closed and we returned home. I prayed that I might be wise and do all I was called to do with a loving, gentle spirit, and not censure or blame any one; but work sweetly the work He, my Saviour, hath sent me to do. Amen."

CHAPTER XXI.

Here no Continuing City.—Her Last Move.—Jamaica a Center.—
Service Performed in Absence of Pastor.—Erection of Church
and Parsonage, 1872.—Her Joy.—Erection of Chapel, 1888.—
Pleasant Memories.—Dedication Hymn.—Sunday-school After-
noon.—Poem.—Visits Whitestone.—Extracts from Diary.—
Northport.—Talks About Jesus.

"FOR here we have no continuing city, but we seek one to come," was said of God's worthies in olden times. They were not dwellers for a long time in any one place. Very largely those who are God's Israel come on in the same line and have a similar experience. Permanence of place in this life more frequently belongs to those who seek their good in this world; who, like the people of old, of whom God said, "Moab hath been at ease from his youth, and he hath settled upon his lees;" while of God's Israel, they are "emptied from vessel to vessel," that their "*scent*" and "*taste*" might be changed to the true standard.

So it was with Nettie. From her birth till within a few years of her death she was one of an itinerant family, whose removals were made by rule and frequent. We have often heard her say, "There is no spot in all the many places where I have lived of which I could say, as I have heard others, 'This is my home; here I was born, and here I spent my childhood.' Mine, with my dear father and mother, has, indeed, been a pilgrimage. I have often desired a more permanent home, but I have never reached it."

One more move, the third time back to Jamaica; and this was to be her resting-place until called to her permanent abode beyond the scenes of mortal strife. It appears providential that these last and most useful years of her life should be spent where some of the most interesting events of her life had taken place. From this home, as a radiating center, she could more easily respond to the many calls made for her service and labor.

The church here held her in the highest esteem and honor. Very often, in the absence of the pastor, she, by special invitation, would take the Sabbath services, and in her own loving way carry them through, very much to the edification of the church and people; while, as they listened and heard, they "took knowledge of her that she had been with Jesus and learned of him."

During the year 1872 the society in Jamaica commenced the erection of a new church and parsonage. A strange providence had provided and held a loca-

11

tion, the most inviting and beautiful in the whole village, until they were able to build. In the erection of this new church Nettie took a deep interest, and with her husband contributed an amount that was large beyond their means.

It was a gift that cost a sacrifice to the givers, but they esteemed this church as a part of their inheritance, and so took large stock in the undertaking. When the beautiful edifice was completed and dedicated none rejoiced more than she, and with others her prayer arose much like the prayer of Solomon on the dedication of the temple : " Now therefore arise, O Lord God, unto thy resting-place, thou, and the ark of thy strength : let thy priests, O Lord God, be clothed with salvation, and let thy saints rejoice in goodness."

Upon her return to Jamaica after two or three years the society erected a new and commodious chapel. This was done to accommodate the growing numbers attending Sabbath-school and prayer-meetings. It was Nettie's privilege to be present during its construction and completion. Its opening and dedication was a time of rejoicing, second only to the completion of the church.

None entered more fully into the joy of the occasion than she; to her many pleasant memories clustered around the old chapel, yet her faith invested the new one with such importance that the old "had no glory by reason of the glory that in this new chapel was to excel."

The following dedication hymn was composed by her, and sung at the opening service:

> "In this new chapel let us feel,
>   As Israel did of old,
> That God is here, the place to fill
>   With wondrous gifts untold.
>
> "As when upon the mercy-seat
>   Thy glory did appear,
> So, Lord, with us, thy children, meet
>   When we are gathered here.
>
> "Come in this place; O, come to stay,
>   While years and ages move;
> From glory's height now let a ray
>   Come beaming from above.
>
> "May many souls here find the Lord,
>   To justify and save;
> And prove the fullness of his word,
>   As when his Son he gave."

The afternoon services by the Sabbath-school exceeded, if possible, the morning occasion. All the apartments of the large building were full and crowded. The exercises were partly memorial. It was the blending of the past with the present.

In the minds of many who participated these could not be separated. The tears of joy that gathered in

many eyes were mingled with tears of sadness because
of the past. This feeling of joy and sorrow finds
true expression in the following verses composed by
Nettie and read on the occasion :

"We've left the old house for the new,
    Though memory lingers still,
And brings full many a scene to view,
    And forms we loved so well.

"There gathered then a little flock,
    Full eighteen years ago,
On Sabbath eve, at six o'clock,
    The way of life to know.

"They used to meet to join in prayers
    And praise to God above;
But some now crowns of glory wear—
    They've reached their home of love.

"Dear brother *Frank* has gained his rest,
    And *Sadie*, too, has gone,
To take their place among the blest,
    And sing around the throne.

"And *Mott*, who, in his early life,
    Found Jesus as his friend,
Long since has ceased this earthly strife
    For joys that never end.

"Sweet songs of praise they there did sing,
    As, 'O, come, angel band,'
Or, 'To the cross of Christ I cling,'
    'We stand on Jordan's strand.'

" While faithful leaders led the way
 God filled them with his love;
They used to sing and shout and pray,
 And talk of things above.

" And souls rejoiced in sins forgiven,
 And sought for higher grace;
It came, and turned their night to heaven,
 While Jesus showed his face.

" So while the changing years have flown
 God blesses still this hour;
And now we pray, O, Jesus, come,
 On us thy Spirit pour."

We do not wonder that Nettie should have a thrilling interest in these services. A goodly number of those present as well as those who had passed on, having gained their crowns, were her spiritual children begotten in Christ, and beloved by her as a "nurse cherisheth her children." The occasion will long be remembered because of her presence and work, until the general and joyful meeting takes place with the "church of the firstborn" in heaven. The following appeared in the village paper:

"THE MEMORIAL SERVICE

of the young people's meeting, held on Sunday evening last in the lecture-room of the Methodist Episcopal church, was very well attended and was a very interesting meeting throughout. Mrs. Nettie

Hill Weeden presided, and Mrs. Frances Hill Johnson assisted at the organ. After about fifteen minutes service of song, prayer was offered, and then Mrs. Weeden addressed the meeting, giving a concise statement of the organization of the meeting in 1870, the outcome of a great revival that took place that year. Ten young converts first met, and since that the numbers have increased until the meetings held every Sunday evening are looked forward to with great anticipation and profit. The reading of the 'memorial roll' was very affecting as name after name was mentioned who had been faithful in life and died in full hope of heaven. Remarks were also made by John B. Hopkins, John C. Acker, D. J. Weeden, Mrs. Holland, Mrs. French, and others, all bearing on the subject of early conversion and full consecration to Christian life.

"Meetings are held every Sunday evening and all are invited."

This letter was written to her father, at that time in Florida. It lovingly refers to some of those saved and crowned, and will be read with much interest:

"Jamaica, L. I., February 22, 1887.

"My Precious Father: What is the matter? I fear you are sick. More than two weeks have passed since you have written in answer to three letters I have sent you. I am looking for one by to-night's mail. I hope I may not be disappointed. I almost feel hurt with the postmaster, who has so often spoken the tiresome word to me, ' Not any thing to-day.'

"This day celebrates Washington's birth:

> "' The flag of the free,
> O, long may it wave
> O'er the land that can boast
> Of a Washington's grave.'

"Winter, cold and uncomfortable, is yet with us; and now, while writing this, the snow and sleet breaks upon the window, while without I hear the almost ceaseless twitter of the sparrows that seem to see something even in the leaden sky to tell them spring is coming. Since its beginning the snow has continued to spread its white mantle upon the earth. Pleasant will it be when spring comes to gladden our hearts, to break winter's icy bands; then nature will pass into the lovely green, with leaves, buds, and flowers; all will seem changed, only the mark of another year will remain with us. Yesterday our dear Doll passed the twenty-sixth mile-stone of her journey. Last week I marked my forty-third, and should he live until May, dear Clint will reach his twentieth.

"How suggestive the thought, 'We are passing away.' Even '*baby Clint*' is now a man out on the great ocean of life. What will be his history? Long years since I received the assurance that he would be saved, and I yet hold to the promise, 'What things soever ye desire, when ye pray, believe that ye receive them, and ye *shall* have them.' I do believe, and therefore rejoice. Yesterday the remains of Libbie Ryder—now Mrs. Gracy—were laid to rest. She was converted and joined the church during your pastorate in Jamaica. A dear friend recently said to me, 'That was a wonderful revival.' Let me call to mind a few that were then converted that have since passed on to their reward; and besides, the strength of the church here to-day consists in those who were brought in at that time by conversions principally, though a few were received by letter.

"First, leading the list, was little Tany Remsen, the youngest member of the church. He went home singing and rejoicing in his Saviour. Sadie Morrell, sweet girl, said when dying, 'I love Allie,' her husband, 'and my dear child, but I love Jesus more;' thus passing away in holy triumph. Sadie Baylis, so quiet and gentle when passing, put her arms around my neck and simply said, 'I love Jesus;' and near the crossing sang, 'Fully persuaded, Jesus is mine,' and breathed her life out on the bosom of the Saviour. And you remember poor blind Eliza; she was taken to Barnum Island, the county house; from thence she went up to the palace of a King. So you see, my dear father, how wondrously your work was blessed in Jamaica; and I have no doubt could I return to other places as I have here, I would find similar results. Praise God, you have scattered the good seed, and in many instances it is already garnered. And now I must close, with much love and kisses. I am, my dear father, Your affectionate child,

"NETTIE."

Receiving a pressing invitation to visit Whitestone from the Rev. Samuel Gurney, pastor of the Methodist Episcopal church, she went. It was our privilege to accompany her there. She felt a strong desire to visit that place, for there she had once resided, and among those friends she had formed strong attachments. Moreover, the place had in her mind a sacredness, for there her sister was born that brought a new dawning to her life. While there she was a stranger to the love of Christ, and the most of her young friends and associates were of the same kind. Now she much desired to return and tell those friends of the love of Jesus. On December 29, 1888, she went. The following is from her diary:

"Sunday morning my dear father preached from Joshua 4. 6, 'What mean ye by these stones?' I followed with an exhortation, and 'sang for Jesus.' In the afternoon I visited the Sabbath-school, where once

I was a member.   I earnestly entreated the scholars to
give their hearts to the Lord in their youth.   There was
a deep religious feeling.   I asked all who desired to lead
a new life, giving themselves to the Saviour, to make
it manifest.   Nearly the whole school responded, and
gathered around the altar and front seats kneeling in
prayer.   It was a scene of deepest interest ; quite a
number found there a personal interest in Jesus as
their Saviour.   In the evening, after father had
preached, I followed in words of exhortation.   My
heart was deeply drawn out for the dear people.   I
called upon the members to give themselves fully to
God ; they quickly responded, and the altar was filled
while the earnest prayer ascended, 'Create in *me* a
clean heart, O God.'   Thus passed this delightful
Sabbath.   Purity of heart and power to work seemed
to be the great desire of the church.

"The next night was New Year's eve, and watch-
night services were appointed.   Father returned home
in the morning ; I was pressed to remain.   In the
afternoon we held a service in the church, and a most
delightful time was experienced.

"At nine o'clock the services commenced.   The
Lord was present indeed ; many sought for pardon,
while not a few earnestly sought the blessing of a
clean heart.   A blessed shower of grace seemed to
rest upon this dear people and upon Brother Gurney,

their beloved pastor, whose heart is deeply endued by the Spirit of Christ, and who grandly leads on his flock to higher experiences. Tuesday morning returned home weary in body but rejoicing in spirit. Found all the dear ones well."

During the succeeding weeks, as we follow her, we find her engaged in the work of all others she loved, responding to the many calls from pastors to come and assist them. At Springfield, thence to Northport, where for two weeks she engaged afternoon and evening in revival work, and here the Lord was graciously present to save. We will let her briefly describe what followed:

"January 12, went with my husband to Northport by invitation from Brother J. S. Stansbury, the pastor. On Sunday morning he preached, after which I spoke. I held before the people the work to be done. I told them I had come to them from another part of the Lord's vineyard and, perhaps, was a stranger to many; yet now I was one with them in 'heart and spirit joined.' I spoke of my sainted grandparents, who resided, worked, and died but a short distance from where we were now engaged; I told them they were Methodists of the old stock and believed 'in the power,' and I wanted to follow in the same line, trusting for success in their God and Saviour.

"In the afternoon visited the Sabbath-school, and

invited all who desired to become Christians to come forward; some responded and came. So deep was the feeling that many cried aloud, weeping for their sins as if their hearts were breaking. In the evening I spoke at length on the promise made by the Saviour to the disciples just previous to his ascension into heaven, 'But ye shall receive power, after that the Holy Ghost is come upon you,' etc. Several came forward desirous of realizing the promise of power from on high—one seeker for pardon. This meeting with its results I pass over into the hands of my heavenly Father. I don't know what will be the measure of success; I leave it with him who hath said, 'My word that goeth forth out of my mouth, it shall not return unto me void.'

"Now begins another day for Jesus. Received from friends a call in the morning; had an interesting conversation about Christian work. As the afternoon was near at hand made some preparation therefor and went to the church. I resumed the subject of 'power,' and there followed truly a half hour with Jesus. I saw the harvest blooming and ripening, and encouraged the church to believe it. O, how few are the laborers. Went from the church to see a sick lady.

"Evening. Brother Stansbury led a praise service, after which I spoke on, 'For the Son of man is come to seek and save them that are lost.' Many came forward as seekers; several testified to the wondrous power of Jesus to save. Some testimonies were from converts recently converted at Dix Hills. So ends another day. Lord, I pass it with all its results over to thee. Only work in me and through me, and keep on blessing thy people.

"Another day commences. 'O Lord, revive thy work.' In the afternoon I spoke of our Lord's words, 'If any man will be my disciple, let him deny himself and take up his cross daily, and follow me.' I told them a little of my own experience in cross-bearing; alluded to the woman who was converted last night; also to a young friend of mine who, rejecting the cross, came to deny the Saviour. The Lord greatly blessed us. My soul longs for the conversion of sinners. In the evening a large number present; I cried to the people, 'Almost thou persuadest me to be a Christian.' I warned them to 'flee from the wrath to come.' I went out in the congregation, urging the backslider to return again and those whose evidence was unsatisfactory not to rest until they found a clear title. Five presented themselves at the altar. None desired to be cleansed; at least, all shrank from making it manifest. I earnestly besought the Lord to come in power and save to the uttermost and to convert sinners."

We will not further follow by detail the meetings; it seemed at times that victory would be reached, then partial defeat. But as we follow her work the cloud continued to arise until the shower came and many were saved, concerning which she says:

"After speaking on, 'And they were all filled with the Holy Ghost,' I asked all who wanted this divine filling to come forward, and the church came in mass; sinners also came, blessed testimonies were given! Thus ended another week for the Master—victory on the Lord's side! Praise his holy name!

"Sabbath morning. A spirit of consecration fills my soul to-day.

"Friday has come. It is my last day in Northport. To-morrow I return home. In the evening I spoke once more about the 'well of living water.' The Lord was wondrously present; the altar was filled with those seeking pardon and many panting for purity. Some were converted. Praise the Lord, O, my soul, for these two weeks and results. Amen."

These extracts are briefly made; they disclose, however, her real and holy longings for the salvation of sinners and the sanctification of believers. Those who witnessed her spirit and labors on such occasions saw how deeply she was consecrated to this work. Nothing would satisfy her desires but a revival, and when this was attained her joy was full. No general going through the fire of battle to victory was ever more elated. To her the struggle, the toil, the doubts and failures would all be forgotten as victory rang along the line of God's host. To her it was always an hour of triumph, and she could sing:

> "When Satan appears to stop up our path,
> And fills us with fears, we triumph by faith;
> He cannot take from us, though oft he has tried,
> The heart-cheering promise, 'The Lord will provide.'"

The following is one of her "talks about Jesus," a subject most dear to her heart. His love, sympathy, and condescension were themes upon which she delighted to dwell.

If in her simple and earnest manner she could present the divine Man as a brother to love, who could enter into the full experience of our sufferings, she seemed to touch the highest and sweetest chord of her nature.

"Jesus Wept."—John 11. 35.

"This is the shortest verse in the Bible. Composed of only two words, and concerning which the great commentator, Dr. Adam Clarke, says, 'The least verse in the Bible, and *yet inferior to none.*' Without this little verse the book would be unfinished and incomplete.

"Do you ask why? We answer, it speaks of both heaven and earth. 'Jesus.' That name represents heaven. 'Wept.' This word represents earth. Nowhere are they brought closer together. 'Jesus,' the highest joy of heaven; 'wept,' the deepest vale of earthly sorrow. A striking contrast, yet having a strange and mysterious blending.

> " ' The Son of God in tears
> Let wondering angels see.'

" Jesus is the *highest name*, the only name

> " ' That charms our fears,
> That bids our sorrows cease;
> 'Tis music in the sinner's ears,
> 'Tis life, and health, and peace.'

" ' Jesus.' The name is a *synonym of power.* ' Go tell John the things ye now see and hear. The blind receive their sight, and the lame walk, the lepers are cleansed, and the deaf hear, the dead are raised up, and the poor have the Gospel preached to them.' I hear his voice, ' Young man, I say unto thee, arise,' and a widowed mother embraces her only son brought back from the realms of death. He makes clay of spittle and anoints the eyes of a blind man, and light penetrates the sightless eyeballs. He touches the loathsome leper, and health courses through the fevered veins. ' Jesus ' is the

" Joy-giver.

" Well do I remember how the fathers and mothers used to sing,

> " ' His name yields the richest perfume,
> And sweeter than music his voice.'

And it is true to-day as it was forty or eighteen hundred years ago. There rises before my mind a scene on the Sea of Galilee. A company of men go forth to their toil; they are fishermen, with faces bronzed, hands hardened, and backs bent. They cast their nets. They bring them to the shore. No fish! Since the setting sun, far into the night, have these toilers wrought. 'That night they caught nothing.' How it illustrates much of human endeavor. Now they leave their boats and begin to 'wash their nets.' A conversation might have been heard; perhaps Peter is the first speaker: 'This has been a discouraging night; see, our nets are wearing out by constant throwing.' Another, perhaps James, speaks: 'That barrel of meal at home is nearly empty.' One more speaks; it might have been Andrew: 'Dear little Moses is at home sick; I thought to have taken him something from the sea to tempt his appetite.' Now the waves dash around them, and laugh at their disappointment, while the morning cloud throws a darker shadow upon those weary toilers as they finish their worthless task.

" But I see a crowd of people on the shore, anxious to behold the wonderful Man and to hear his words. Upon the beautiful Gennesaret the sun had often shone with golden colors; but never before was there such an exhibition of unearthly brightness. The Sun

12

of Righteousness had there risen to illumine the scene with celestial glory.

"Along with the multitude his eye took in the 'two boats,' and the weary fishermen as well. His omniscience had not lost sight of their disappointed look and empty net. He saw it all. Now coming to Simon's boat he entered it, and 'bid him thrust out a little from the land,' and that little skiff became a *pulpit* from which he was to preach to the people. A floating *Bethel*, out from which the gospel net was to be thrown. Of all the craft, great and small, that have floated on ocean, sea, or river since the world began, none has been so ennobled or admired as Simon's, while Jesus from its sides taught the people on the shore. But see! the eastern sky is gilded with the beautiful rays of the rising sun, and the eager crowds are anxiously waiting to hear, while Simon holds the little ship to her anchorage. The central figure is Jesus. He preaches, but the sermon is not reported. Through the minds of those disappointed men there doubtless were varied thoughts; to all of them rest was needed; possibly there might begin to creep over their senses a drowsy stupor; but the magnetic voice of the divine Preacher dispels their lethargy while its tones thrill their hearts. The time for preaching is now past and the moment for action come. 'Launch out into the deep and let

down your nets for a draught,' is the command.
'Blessed are they who hear his word, *and do it*.' A
great many are only hearers; they are like those
'who, beholding their natural face in the glass, go
their way, and straightway forget what manner of
persons they are.' The word and opportunity that
summon them to action are all important. Will the
disciples heed them? Wearied and exhausted nature
and a fruitless experience might cause them to hesitate. 'What's the use? The present can be no better
than the past.' Ah, dear friends, we may not be
governed in our present duties by our past experience. It may have been successful, or barren of results. Faith turns away from all these and looks to
Him, the Promiser, alone. 'Master,' says Simon, 'we
have toiled all the night, and have taken nothing;
nevertheless, at thy word I will let down the net.'
Because thou commandest it, that settles every question of duty. The omniscient eye of Jesus beholds
the school of fish sweeping along the shore toward
the boat; the net is cast; it is the opportune moment, and human effort is supplemented with divine
supply.

"RESULT,

'a multitude of fishes,' yet some further trial of
faith: 'and their net brake.' Tie it up, and pull on.
'The ships begin to sink.' Bail them out, and pull in

the harder. But they land the fish. 'Well done, Simon, you have succeeded splendidly.' Ah, how natural that poor human nature should take credit to themselves. In our successes we sometimes do this; but Peter did not. In the presence of this manifestation of Godlike power Peter saw his failings and infirmities, and cried out, 'Depart from me, for I am a sinful man, O Lord.' Astonishment fill all their hearts. This wonderful draught of fishes seems to come in the natural way, yet to them it was all supernatural. 'It is the Lord's doings, and is marvelous in our eyes.' O, when, dear Christian workers, shall we cease to depend upon ourselves? When shall we fully take Jesus's word, with its promises, and believe, to the salvation of body and soul?

"But the preaching has ceased, though not its effects. The crowd that had hung with breathless interest upon his word now take their way to their homes; the aged and young who alike had followed him from desert to lake. Since early light they had seen his form and listened to such words 'as never man spake.'"

EARLY SERVICES.

"Who will attend an early-morning meeting? The people did when John Wesley was to preach. In the life of Jesus there were anxious, hungry hearts. I imagine I hear one say, 'I want to hear Jesus to-morrow morning.' The careful one says, ' You are too old and feeble to go to the desert ; ' but the reply is, ' It is my first opportunity ; I may never have another. It is the hour of my life; I will take my rest. Call me early, for I must hear Jesus.' And the little child says, ' May I go and hear Jesus ? ' The careful one says, ' You are too young, my dear, to understand these things, and the crowd will injure my darling.' But the sobbing child is only soothed by the promise, ' You shall go with grandpa and hear Jesus.' Thus homes are left; the highway while it is yet dark presents a strange scene. Age and childhood alike forget their infirmities, their weakness, and frailties. Words for soul and body are to fall from the lips of the sacred Teacher. They behold his form, they listen, and tears fall from aged, aching eyes while they respond, ' He hath raised up for us a horn of salvation.' ' God hath visited his people.' And thus to-day is Jesus the ' joy-giver.' No words so sweet as his, no peace like the peace he gives, and ' your heart shall rejoice, and your joy no man taketh from you.'

" ' JESUS WEPT.'

" This brings us to the earth side. ' Made an high-priest like unto his brethren.' Tears from Jesus show how tenderly he puts himself in sympathy with us. He became the ' Man of sorrows.' The ' Lily of the

Valley' is bruised and crushed. Human woe and sorrow lie heavy upon his heart; for

> " ' He, in the days of sinful flesh,
> Poured out strong cries and tears;
> And in his measure feels afresh
> What *every member* bears.'

Let us to-day sweep aside the drapery of nearly nine-teen centuries, and take ourselves to the sorrowful home in Bethany. The doors are shut and fastened. Where are the inmates? ' Gone to the grave to weep there.' Let us follow; with the group that stand around a new-made tomb we join ourselves. With sorrowful countenances and tearful eyes, they are the two bereaved and broken-hearted sisters. An only brother gone! The staff broken. But from these we turn our eyes to that central figure, around whose form there gathers a deeper interest, while

> " 'Majestic sweetness sits enthroned upon his brow.'

What brings him to this place of burial? Perhaps this will answer the question. 'Jesus wept.' He felt deepest sympathy for that broken home. But why did he tarry so long? 'Could not this Man which opened the eyes of the blind have caused that even this man should not have died?' Yes, he could have stayed the dark-winged messenger of death, and held Lazarus in life; but his death would bring a greater good to that family and the world than his life. The world has been enriched beyond measure by that brother's death. Jesus does not always explain his reasons and plans. Often he throws across the scene a veil. 'What I do now thou knowest not, but they shall know hereafter.' But here he removes the veil. 'I am glad for your sakes I was not there, to the *intent ye may believe*.' Out of that death and broken home was borne the sweetest truth that has fallen upon sorrowing humanity; as necessary to-day as then, for there are always broken hearts.

> " ' This earth is a sorrowful stage,
> A valley of weeping and woe.'

And Jesus yet stands by open graves and in desolate homes and repeats the welcome tidings, 'I am the resurrection and the life.' To those thus sorrowing I would this morning repeat the question, 'Believest thou this?' Let us learn, then, to lean our aching heads upon his bosom, who wept as a man, and by and by he will speak as a God. Then will those who are now held under death's dominion 'come forth!'

> " ' Jesus wept! those tears are over,
> But his heart is still the same;
> Kinsman, Friend, and elder Brother,
> Is his everlasting name.
> Saviour, who can love like thee?
> Gracious One of Bethany.

" ' When the pangs of trial seize us,
   When the waves of sorrow roll,
I will lay my head on Jesus,
   Pillow of the troubled soul.
      Surely none can feel like thee,
      Weeping One of Bethany.

" ' Jesus wept! and still in glory,
   He can mark each mourner's tear;
Living to retrace the story.
   Of the hearts he solaced here.
      Lord, when I am called to die,
      Let me think of Bethany.

" ' Jesus wept! that tear of sorrow
   Is a legacy of love;
Yesterday, to-day, to-morrow,
   He the same doth ever prove.
      Thou art all in all to me,
      Living One of Bethany.' "

CHAPTER XXII.

A True Child of Abraham.—Scope of Prayers.—Faith in Promises.
—Rev. S. F. Johnson.

"THESE all died in faith" was declared of God's ancient worthies; and their true successors are many. They are those who, hearing the words of the Master, believe in and follow him. "He that believeth on me, as the Scriptures hath said, out of his belly shall flow rivers of living water. But this spake he of the Spirit, which they that believe on him should receive." This is the legitimate outcome of true faith—a fullness of God in the soul that will flow out from them to bless others, like refreshing rivers in a thirsty land. Paul, in writing to the Thessalonian Church, declares that he remembered without ceasing "their work of faith."

No one becoming acquainted with Nettie's life and experience can fail to see that she was a true child of Abraham. She *believed God*, and her faith made itself manifest. It was a true, working faith. Naturally she was trustful and confiding; the word and promises of her friends were largely believed and accredited, and it required a large failure to shake her confidence. Her faith and trust in God and his word was strong and abiding. What he had spoken she believed would come to pass ; hence she was accustomed to carry all her wants and desires to Him who had promised. Her prayers embraced a wider scope than her spiritual wants. Somehow she had come to think that her Lord had promised to care for and bless the body as well ; hence her petitions took in all temporalities—matters relating to body and soul—life, health, friends, and substance. And there were times when God did unfold himself to her as a wonderful helper in time of need. Special answers to prayer came to her sometimes in such a manner as to fill her soul with wonder and widen the scope of her faith and love.

Faith and prayer were her great courts of appeal, where every case must be brought and tried. We do not think she was presumptuous. If there were conditions to be observed or means to be used in connection with the fulfillment of the promise, she took them fully into the account and cheerfully performed what related to the human side. " I believe," she was wont to say, " what God has promised he will perform. I cannot think for a moment that my precious Saviour meant to deceive us when he said, ' What things soever ye desire, when ye pray, believe that ye receive them, and ye shall have them.' "

Simply and in a child-like manner she accepted the statement, and trusted in him for the fulfillment of her desires. One instance we call to mind that occurred some three years since. It will serve to illustrate the strength and simplicity of her faith, which, resting upon the word of divine truth, became importunate and even bold. The Rev. Samuel F. Johnson, a superannuated member of the New York East Conference, was at that time residing in Rockville Center, Long Island. For several months his health had been failing; his case was pronounced an incurable one. At this time he was confined to his bed with but little hope of any change for the better. His physician and friends thought him near the end of his mortal journey. He was desirous that a few Christian friends should visit him. There were invited Rev. Sidney K. Smith, Rev. T. M. Terry, Nettie, and her father. These, responding to the call, met at his house. Lying upon his couch, wasted and pale, he cordially greeted us. He said: "I have sent for you, dear friends, to come and see me. 1 desire you should pray with and for me. I don't know just what form your petitions will take; I want you to be directed by the Holy Spirit. I think I desire only the will of God to be done, yet I feel drawn out to say, ask God in behalf of this poor body. **Pray for my healing.** I frankly confess I have not the faith to lay hold of the promise that relates to physical healing, but I want you to pray that the mind of God may be known." The case seemed to stand thus: Our dear brother, though prepared and willing to die, desired to be raised up, if thereby God might be glorified.

Our first inquiry was, "Is there any word of God applicable to this case upon which we may stand?" One of the number turned to Jas. 5. 14, 15, and read: "Is any sick among you? let him call for the elders of the church; and let them pray over him, anointing him with oil in the name of the Lord: and the prayer of faith shall save the sick, and the Lord shall raise him up." Then, turning to the words of Christ found in Mark 11. 24, "Therefore I say unto you, What things soever ye desire, when ye pray, believe that ye receive them, and ye shall have them." In this solemn business before us not one desired to tread upon forbidden ground. To begin, we could only ask, May there not be cases where God permits his people to pray for the healing of the body? If so, does this particular one come within the scope of his promise?

In great humility we began by asking God to show us his mind and help. As we drew near to him he came near to us. As prayer continued the petitions offered seemed to arise above the realm of doubt, and it appeared as if God was about to be honored in the healing of his servant.

"Can you fully trust God to do this work, losing sight of the medicines and stimulants you so long have used, and take him as your healer?"

The sick man could only respond, "Lord, I believe; help thou my unbelief." Just at this point, under a wonderful inspiration, Nettie said:

"I feel deeply impressed that you men of God should perform all the conditions of this promise. The word says, 'Let them pray over him, anointing him with oil in the name of the Lord.'" Then, turning to us, she seemed to speak with authority as she said: "Pa, you must do this."

Under the most solemn impressions of the divine presence we feared to proceed, yet dared not refuse. We gathered around his bed, and while there a cloud of glory filled the room and permeated all our hearts. In our life we have never witnessed such a scene or seemed to stand so close to God. We cannot think of it at this distant day without feelings of holy awe and sweet heavenly peace. Our hands were laid upon the sick one; further than this we did not go. Just here there was an evident failure.

Brother S. K. Smith, one of the number, has expressed to us a regret since that memorable occasion. "I was," he says, "deeply impressed at the time that we should obey the full requirement of the promise, and not only lay hands upon and pray for him, but also anoint him in the name of the Lord. I have deeply regretted since at that solemn point we failed to do it."

As to the results of that interview, they were not complete, though astonishing. There came unusual strength to our brother; he sat up in the bed, and for many days and even weeks he rallied and walked about, and the following Sabbath went to church. His physician and friends were amazed. He was evidently in the condition of the blind man, who, looking up, said, "I see men as trees walking," and only needed the additional touch of an all-restoring faith to be made perfectly whole. After a few weeks he suffered a relapse, and passed away triumphantly to his heavenly home.

In summing up this whole circumstance, in which our dear Nettie took such a prominent part, and whose faith seemed to grasp the prize, we have been led to ask, Were we deceived? Was it a failure? By no means. To this day we firmly believe God honored the measure of faith of that hour in his convalescence and partial recovery. But for reasons only known to himself he withheld from us the completeness of healing. Might we not have been responsible for this? In olden times God spake to Joash, King of Israel, by the mouth of Elisha his prophet, when the king had smitten with arrows but three times:

"Thou shouldst have smitten five or six times; then hadst thou smitten Syria, until thou hadst consumed it. Whereas thou shalt smite Syria but thrice." The king had partial conquest, but it was not full, owing to the fewness of the number of his strokes.

We shall be greatly surprised at the number of our partial victories and defeats when, in the great future, we shall be permitted to see and understand the causes of such failures and defeats.

God gave us enough of success and victory to show us how willing he was to honor the " effectual fervent prayer " and "faith" in his promise, withholding when and where we fail to obey him implicitly. " As thy faith, so shall it be done unto thee." From this there has never been any shrinkage, and never will be so long as our faithful Promiser lives.

In relating the above we have dwelt more at length than we otherwise should, because we have always felt that Nettie was an important actor in that remarkable experience; and that beyond the physical benefit that may have come to the sick one there was experienced by those who participated a blessing of exceeding value, the memory of which is precious to this day.

CHAPTER XXIII.

Anxiety for the Salvation of Others.—Constant Testimony to Higher Grace.—Letters.—From Nettie to Mamie.—From a Young Man.—From a Young Lady.—Correspondence Helped Many.—To the Dear Ones at Home.

DURING the few last years of Nettie's life her soul was more and more drawn out in desire for the salvation of others. Having tasted the delight of pardoned sin she most earnestly desired others to enjoy the same. Added to this she gave constant testimony to the "higher grace of full salvation." And in this there was no uncertain sound. She saw and believed it to be the privilege of the newly converted child of God to enter into this rest, hence she at once urged upon them the duty of entire consecration and supreme trust in Christ the "mighty to save." Nor did her walk conflict with her testimony; with the two there was a beautiful harmony that carried conviction, so that many said, "She has been with Jesus, and learned of him."

Between herself and those who through her instrumentality were brought to the Saviour there was a warmth and attachment that reveals itself in letters received by her. A few we insert here. They show in the simplicity of their young experience how dearly they loved her who, under God, had been made the instrument of their salvation.

" *October* 14, 1888.

" DEAR MRS. WEEDEN : I am still trusting in the Lord Jesus Christ, and always shall. I feel he is with me all the time. The sweet songs of Jesus that you sang are in my mind all the while. Write me soon. From one that loves you dearly. L. C. E."

The following is from a young convert, a girl of twelve years :

" I thought I would write you a few lines to let you know how I am getting along in the Christian life. Since I gave my heart to Jesus I have been very happy. I have been trusting him all the while. He cares for me and keeps me, and I will trust him to the end of my life and then go home, for Jesus has a crown for me. My dearest friend, I am praying for you every day, that Jesus will help you in your work. I hope you will come here in September, when the converts are taken into full membership. It makes me happy whenever I see you. Ever since returning from camp-meeting I have been thinking about you and Jesus, because you are my best friends. O, how

13

much I should like to see you again; your looks are before me as if you were present.   From

"Mamie S."

The following is from a young man converted while she was laboring at A——:

"Sister Weeden: I am still on the way to heaven. Jesus is my Saviour and friend. I cannot write much, but when I see you I can tell you much more. I have neither brother nor sister in this world, but I feel that you are indeed a sister to me; but for you I now would be a wanderer in this world without Jesus.   I praise him that he sent you to A——; but for that I would be drifting I know not where. 'God be with you till we meet again.' I remain your true brother in Christ,   C. S."

This from a young lady, also a convert:

"My Dear Mrs. Weeden: I received your lovely letter containing card and photograph.   I cannot tell you how pleased I am with it, it is so like your own sweet self.   How good the Lord is to me to give me so many kind, loving friends.   This is, you know, the week of prayer; there are meetings every night; a delightful one was held last evening.   God seemed so near.

"Ever yours,

"M. Y. W. H."

The following letters were written to Mamie S——, the convert of twelve years of age, and by request sent from her to us. Gladly we give them a place in this memorial:

"JAMAICA, January 4, 1889.

"To MY DEAR FRIEND MAMIE: Your letter with verses, also your Christmas token, was received with much pleasure. Every time I look at the gift I think of Mamie and know she loves me as I love her. I have been absent from home, engaged in the Lord's work, and have seen precious ones converted. In a few days I go again, to be absent for some time. Although absent from home, I am happy, because I see souls saved. A dear young boy gave his heart to God about a year ago—this week he died; so, you see, not only do the old die, but the young as well. It is well to be ready. How do you get along in your Christian life? Does Jesus save and make you happy? Do you still bear your cross? Does the light yet shine? How are the rest getting along?* Remember me in much love to all the dear friends. Write soon. Lovingly your sister in Christ,

"NETTIE HILL WEEDEN."

The following was written by her only about four weeks before her death to the same:

---

* Alluding to the young converts.

"JAMAICA, September 5, 1889.

"MY DEAR MAMIE: Your very welcome letter received. I am sorry you have been sick. I hope by this time you have fully recovered. I expected to see you at Merrick, but was disappointed. The past summer has been to me a very pleasant one. Husband and I first attended the grove meeting at Dix Hills; thence we went to Merrick, and from there to Ocean Grove. During this time Jesus has been with me, and helped me to tell the "wonderful story" of his power to save, and I have heard many others tell the same. I am so glad my little Mamie loves Jesus yet; I pray you may love him always. If so, you will live with him forever. He died for you, so you must live for him. If you walk in his light, then it will shine upon you, and at last his glory will be yours. One of the sweet hymns I heard sung at Ocean Grove, in that large temple near the sea, is called "The Haven of Rest." And it is true, Mamie, that God's dear ones have rest from many things that give us trouble—such as doubts and fears. It is rest in Jesus; we are not to wait until we die—it is here and now. Let your faith in the precious promises never grow weak—they are yours. How much better to find Jesus in health than to wait until sickness comes. Yesterday I visited a sweet girl; she was lying on her bed with a fever. She was not a Christian; she promised me she would give her heart to Jesus. But, Mamie, it is a poor time. Let us pray for her that she may be saved. And now I will close, as I have other letters to write. With much love to yourself and other friends I met while with you, I am lovingly yours in Jesus, NETTIE HILL WEEDEN."

FROM A YOUNG MAN RECENTLY CONVERTED.

"March 26, 1888.

"CHRISTIAN FRIEND : I take this opportunity to write to you and thank you for the kind prayers you sent up to the good Lord Jesus in my behalf. I feel I cannot be grateful enough to you. It was through you I was led to Jesus, as well as a great many others. I pray every day that the Lord will send his blessing down upon you. You told me of Jesus and his love, and of the reward I should receive if I prove faithful, which, by the grace of Jesus, I mean to do. I hope you will pray for me. Now, Mrs. Weeden, I wish to tell you I never, in all my life, felt so happy as I did on that Sunday night when I yielded my heart to the Lord. The way looked so clear and bright that the greatest sinner in the world, seeing it as I did, would say, Let me live the life of a Christian, not a sinner. O, that they may see it is my earnest prayer. I write this to you, for I feel that I owe you a great debt of gratitude that I can never pay; your kind words and prayers for me in person. I can only pray that the Lord will bless you and strengthen you for evermore.

"A few days ago Satan tempted me, but I went straight to my room and prayed, and the Lord gave me the victory. Mrs. Weeden, I mean to meet you in heaven. If I should never see or hear you more on earth, I desire to see you in that beautiful home over there. At times I can almost see that blessed place, and Jesus so saves me that I feel happy soul and body. The dear Saviour is still converting souls in A——. But I must close.　　　　C. S.

"A——, LONG ISLAND."

The following letter was written by a young lady whose conversion was clear, but who, like many others, suffered her faith to get cold, and by negligence lost her Christian hope.

"*April* 29, 1886.

"DEAR MRS. WEEDEN: Do you remember the caller that came to your house on that stormy morning and asked if she might write to you? Never mind, you can tell when you look at the signature; if my call is forgotten, I am sure my name is not. Dear Mrs. Weeden, I think I came to you on that morning for a twofold purpose. First, to tell you my troubles,

sure of a sympathizing friend, and next to see if the
Mrs. Weeden at meetings and the Mrs. Weeden at
home were the same; and I found they were. You
will pardon me for telling all about myself. I do
not doubt my conversion. It reminds me of the
' lost chord ' you spoke of, so grand and beautiful;
but, Mrs. Weeden, I have tried so hard but cannot
strike it again. It is all darkness.

"I saw so much inconsistency in others I began to
doubt even the existence of God. Does it shock you
that I thus write? . . . I feel I am a poor backslider.
How much I despise myself—to have known his mercy
and love and then to have turned my back upon him!
Where am I standing? I do not know; I only
know this state began by neglect. At school I became interested in my studies and neglected prayer.
In the place where I resided the Methodists were in
the minority and very poor; pride took me away from
my own church to a richer one. . . . Meanwhile I
felt miserable and ill at ease, and now I earnestly
desire forgiveness. But I cannot pray. I attend
meetings and think I will tell the friends how I feel ;
but they seem so happy that it makes the contrast
greater. I read the Bible, and this is the comfort I
get there : ' If any man love not the Lord Jesus Christ '
let him be Anathema, Maran atha ' (cursed of God).
How terrible the thought! The thought of an angry

God follows me even in my dreams. . . . Mrs.
Weeden, pity me, and if possible help me. . . .

" Your anxious   M. G."

The next letter was written by the same person,
who, like Bunyan's Pilgrim, had gotten out of By-
path into the King's Highway again.

" October 19, 1886.

" Mrs. Weeden :

" Dear Friend : I have many times thought of
you since I last saw you. . . . I feel very differently
from the heart-sick girl who wrote you some months
ago. I now have faith in Jesus, and I mean to hold
it fast ; not only because I have so sure a hope of
heaven, but because of the every-day help I receive.
I find it so sweet to trust in Jesus. When my school
troubles me (for I am now teaching) I tell him, and
he takes my burdens. If I feel impatient, I tell my
ever present Friend. O, how could I have lived so
long without him ! Still I am longing for a deeper
draught from the ' well of salvation.' I greatly desire
the experience I hear others speak of, that of entire
sanctification.

" Dear Mrs. Weeden, I am longing to see you ; but
perhaps it is at present impossible. . . . I bid you
good-night and good-bye.

" Your sister,   M. G."

There is much of correspondence found among her papers, coming very largely from those who were helped by her into the kingdom, and many who through her sweet experience and life were assisted to enter " Beulah Land." These are all expressive of Christian affection and gratitude. From her, in return, went out a warmth of love only known to those who lead souls " to righteousness."

To her it was given to say, " For what is our hope or joy or crown of rejoicing? Are not even ye in the presence of our Lord Jesus Christ at his coming? For ye are our glory and joy."

Her home correspondence was without intermission. When absent seldom a week passed without writing to " the dear ones at home." These letters are a treasure to those who sorrow for her absence. They were her heart-deliverances to those of all others most dear to her in this world.

CHAPTER XXIV.

Miscellaneous Papers.—Keeping Step with God.—Tax on Water.—
Not Having on the Wedding Garment.—"This Day shalt Thou be
with Me in Paradise."—"The Poor Ye Have Always with You."
—Nelson.—Hold on to the Grip.

WE here present a few miscellaneous papers,
written hastily, yet preserved and used in her
public ministrations as incident and illustration.
Many such were taken up by her and woven into her
experiences. They were simple, yet practical, and
when spoken were often deeply interesting and
effective.

Keeping Step with God.

" A company of soldiers were passing through the
street. As they went the band played martial airs.
I observed their gay uniform. But what most
attracted my attention was one in citizen's dress, who
as he marched with them kept a *perfect step* with the
company. I thought, If that man breaks step it will
throw the whole company in confusion.

" So Jesus, our great Captain, gives us marching
orders and commands us to ' *walk before him perfectly.*'

" This means keeping step with God. Is it possible ?

Has it been done? Yes; Enoch walked (that is, kept step) with God for three hundred years, and was not; for God took him.

"Abraham was commanded, 'Walk before me.' He marched on, keeping perfect step with God's commandments. When a sacrifice was demanded, though it was 'Isaac, thine only son whom thou lovest,' he gave it, believing God could raise him from the dead, whence also he received him in a figure. When commanded to go forth he started, 'not knowing whither he went.' When division was made of the land he gave the best to his nephew, reserving the poorest for himself, keeping perfect step, not as an angel, but as a man. So may we keep perfect step to the music of his will and word all the days of our lives."

TAX ON WATER.

" Recently husband and I concluded to move. Having secured a house, such an one as would be desirable, we agreed with the owner to lease it upon condition that water should be brought into the building. We had heretofore been obliged to draw it up from a well or obtain it by pumping. In either case it was labor. To get it in the house and simply to turn a faucet, thus easily obtaining a liberal supply, was very desirable. It was done; the connection with the main was made, and a full supply was at hand. But judge

of my surprise when I learned for this favor a yearly
tax had to be paid.

"*Nothing good without cost!* Well, praise God,
there is no tax on the water of life. 'Whosoever
will, let him come and take of the water of life freely.'
'*Without money or price.*'"

Not having on the Wedding Garment.

"Some time since I received an invitation to attend
a wedding. The nuptial ceremony was to take place
in the church. I concluded not to go. It was the
evening of my class, besides, I was weary from the
duties of the day; yet I could not neglect this means
of grace from which I had received so much help and
comfort. Hastily attiring myself I started for the
class-room. On my way I met a throng of people
going to the wedding. I thought, Well, I will just
step in and see the ceremony performed and get a
view of the bride and groom. As I entered I found
the church dimly lighted, and I was met by one of
the ushers, who conducted me up the aisle until I
reached one of the front seats.

"Presently the sexton turned on the side lights.
I now saw I was surrounded by guests who had come
prepared, and were arrayed in apparel befitting the
occasion. As I looked at myself I began to feel
ashamed that I was no better attired. Still, if no more

light should be turned on I might be saved from greater mortification. Delusive hope! for suddenly the great head or center light flashed out and down with almost a dazzling brightness. My mortification became painful. I now could understand as never before the meaning of the Saviour's words, 'How camest thou in, not having on the wedding garment?' How glad I was when the ceremony was over and the lights turned off. It was a relief to go into darkness again.

"But it was only an earthly wedding—that which revealed my unfitness was only gas-light. Thank God, I am getting ready for the 'marriage of the Lamb;' and I need not be improperly clad; for 'Unto the bride was given that she should be clothed in fine linen, pure and white.' That is to be my apparel, and being vested with such robes I shall not only stand the test of the 'side lights,' but when in the presence of an assembled world, and the great Center-light shall flash out, which will be the Lamb himself, I shall not be ashamed nor asked the question, 'Friend, how camest thou in hither, not having on the wedding garment?'"

"IN HIM SHALL ALL THE FAMILIES OF THE EARTH BE BLESSED."

> "Hark! I hear a gentle murmur
> Come stealing on my ear
> Upon the breeze of summer,
> My weary heart to cheer.

" It is a band of pilgrims
    Upon their journey home;
They're chanting heavenly music,
    They're nearing now the throne.

" The first, a sainted father,
    Now leading on the band;
His steps, they do not falter—
    He's bound to Canaan's land.

" He sees the crown of glory
    That fadeth not away,
Prepared for all the faithful
    Amid the realms of day.

" His step grows light and joyous,
    A smile plays o'er his brow,
He whispers, 'Christ is precious,
    And I behold him now.'

" Hark! hear the song he's singing,
    And higher floats the strain:
'Bright ones my crown are bringing,
    And I a kingdom claim.'

" And then a gentle mother
    With triumph joins the song:
' Christ loves me as none other,
    The parting won't be long.

" 'I leave my little children,
    And all I have below;
I'll take my flight to glory,
    And all its raptures know.'

"Just then an angel beckoned,
  And waved a crown of light,
When she an heir was reckon'd
  In mansions pure and bright.

"And soon a loving sister,
  With listening ear attent,
Catches the loud hosanna
  That father, mother sent.

" ' The world seems dark without them,
  The storms are coming fast;
I think I'll go and meet them,
  And sing while ages last.

" 'I leave this robe of mourning
  And take the garment white;
I'll wear a palm of victory,
  And bid farewell to night.'

"And then she shouted, ' Glory!'
  The answering glory came;
A host of ones most holy,
  And Christ the precious Lamb.

" But scarcely had the rustling
  Of their golden pinions ceas'd,
Or the shouting and the waving
  Of the gathering home of sheaves,

" Then a little boy who slumbered,
  The little darling one:
'I in heaven am numbered;
  O, mamma, let me come.

" ' O, take me, blessed Saviour,
   Up to that world of light;
I'll never know of sorrow;
   O, let me take my flight.'

" Just then a golden chariot
   Close to that cradle pressed,
And angels laid the sleeper
   Upon the Saviour's breast.

" Now all the four are singing,
   No ' rocks or storms ' they fear;
But joyous songs they're hymning
   To Christ their Saviour dear.

" The saints of God are calling,
   The Saviour says, ' Well done; '
They're safe at last in glory,
   They are resting 'neath the throne."

" This Day shalt Thou be with Me in Paradise."

" *One* saved in the last hour to show us the possibility, and but one only recorded to impress us with the extreme danger of neglecting salvation until the eleventh hour. Some few months since I became acquainted with Mrs. H. K. In her home we were cordially received and kindly entertained.

" As a wife, mother, and grandparent she was all that could be desired. We shall not soon forget the smile that always greeted us when visiting her home. With an amiable disposition and a loving heart, she threw a ray of sunshine upon the home circle and friends. It was her delight to lighten and help carry the burdens of others. Yet, with all this, we do not think she had fully accepted Christ as her personal Saviour. But with a nature so lovely, she was 'not far from the kingdom of God.' It needed but one touch of the Master's gentle hand to bring her into the fold and make her one of Christ's little ones. That touch, I believe, she subsequently received.

"Some months passed; we heard of her illness, but supposed we should see her again. But in this we were mistaken. One day there came to us the intelligence of her death. It was sudden and startling; throughout the community the news was deeply felt. For weeks she had been ill, but friends thought she might recover. From the first of her illness she thought otherwise; she seemed impressed that this was her last, and so declared to her friends. Her time indeed had come; the light of her life flickered in the socket, then seemed to burn up brightly. While the death angel waited a moment, she whispered, 'I'm going home,' then expired.

"Could we go behind the curtain and analyze those moments and hours of pain and anxiety we should see, doubtless, her heart brought into communion with her Saviour. How much joy it would have afforded us could we have heard her testimony and witnessed the Christian life that would have followed. But as this

14

was not permitted, we do not doubt in her last days
pardon and victory came.

   " 'I'm going home,' our dear one said,
     When in the vale of death;
  While with loving, anxious friends so sad,
     She yielded up her breath.

  " This rapturous thought, 'I'm going home,'
     Illumed her dying hour,
  And brightness from the golden throne
     Its beams of light did pour.

  " When did she find, and where and how,
     Did she the Saviour meet?
  When as a suppliant did she bow
     Before the mercy-seat?

  " We cannot tell—but all alone
     Her cry went up to God;
  He heard and answered—it was done
     According to his word.

  "The anxious hours, the weary strife,
     Led her to earnest prayer,
  And opened up the way of life,
     And bid her enter there.

  " How sweet, could we but hear her say
     That Jesus was her rest;
  But we will wait 'till heaven's day
     Finds her among the blest.

  " Husband and children dear, to-day
     Your wife and mother's gone;
  Take Jesus as 'the life, the way,'
     And say, ' we're going home.'

"Nor wait until the hour of death,
  But seek the Saviour now;
Place on your immortal brows the wreath,
  While you at Calvary bow.

" Begin the never-ending life
  Where sorrow ne'er shall come,
That when you end this weary strife
  You'll sing, ' we're going home.'

" Farewell, dear sister, till we meet
  Around the glorious throne ;
We'll sing the precious notes so sweet,
  Praise God, ' we're going home.'

"Upon the death of Mrs. H. K., November 25, 1887."

"THE POOR YE HAVE ALWAYS WITH YOU."

"Near by my father's home in Huntington there
lived 'Nelson and Lizzie,' an aged colored man and
his wife. Their home was very small and poor and
sadly out of repair, yet they were God's dear children,
and anticipated a better one in the world to come.
During Nelson's last sickness I visited him.   As I
sat by his bedside and talked with him about the
change that would soon come, 'Yes,' said the old man,
as his eye brightened ; 'yes, the karriot is coming.'
After kneeling down I prayed with him and left.   In
a few days, at nearly one hundred years of age, it did
come ; the 'chariot came,' and the poor old colored
man moved into a mansion.

" I expect among the angels
  Nelson's face with joy will shine,
When I meet him by the portals
  At the hallelujah time.

" Hovel, color, all forgotten,
  While in heaven he takes his place,
For his name above is written
  As a sinner saved by grace.

" For the Lord came down from glory,
  And the robe of flesh did wear,
That we all might tell the story,
  And our Saviour's image bear.

"Farewell, neighbor, till I meet you,
  Not in weakness, staff in hand,
For immortal youth awaits you
  In yon bright and sunny land."

HOLD ON TO THE GRIP.

" Riding one day in the cars I met a friend. In our conversation I inquired about her son, who a few years before had fallen and injured his hand so as to disfigure it somewhat. ' It is still so,' said the mother; but with joy beaming in her eye, she added, ' He still retains his grip. He might have had the muscles cut and so have retained a perfect form of hand, but there would be no grip.'

" Well, I thought, how important we retain our 'grip' on God. To do this it will be to make us pe-

culiar in the eyes of the world and perhaps out of
sympathy with it. But to retain our hold on Christ
is most important. The world would sever and cut
this muscle to make us appear like itself. But let us
by all means and at all cost and sacrifice 'hold on to
the grip.' "

CHAPTER XXV.

"Kissing Away Defilement."

THE following has been kindly furnished by the Rev. A. C. Bowdish, D.D.:

" *Rev. Francis C. Hill:*

"My dear Brother: At your earnest solicitation I send you my humble tribute to the memory of your now sainted daughter, Mrs. Nettie Hill Weeden:

" 'Kissing Away Defilement.

" 'our duties.

" ' God's angels drop like grains of gold
Our duties midst life's shining sands,
And from them, one by one, we mold
Our own bright crowns with patient hands.
From dust and dross we gather them;
We *toil and stoop for love's sweet sake*,
To find each worthy act a gem
In glory's kingly diadem,
Which we may daily richer make. '

" The relation of the following story of how 'Sister Nettie' (as she was familiarly called) reached and redeemed a fallen woman was told at the Merrick Camp-meeting, on Long Island, in the fall of 1888. It was at the one o'clock meeting for young people and children. I think the meeting was in her charge. She was speaking of the different 'fruits of the Spirit,' and the one prominent feature of the Spirit's manifestation (to her) was that of charity.

" Her testimony regarding the power of love ; of her keen sense of obligations to divine benevolence ; her firm belief in the sure connection between her love for God and her love for the souls of men, and this love for the latter growing out of her faith in God and her hope of immortality and her sweet experience of entire sanctification ; her constraining love for the poor and outcast of earth ; her hearty willingness to cherish this principle in her heart—a principle so comprehensive as to take in the eternal interests of men and reaching out beyond the narrow limits of this life—her steadfast, immovable zeal, leading her into all the many lanes of life to 'abound in the work of the Lord,' was so full of pathos, and yet told with such commendable sweetness and simplicity, that all felt the power of the divine One resting upon them. And then, quoting the words of Faber,

> " ' 'Tis not enough to weep *my* sins,
> 'Tis but *one* step to heaven ;
> When I am kind to others
> Then I know myself forgiven,'

she related the following touching experience as coming to her in the work of the Woman's Christian

Temperance Union Society of Jamaica, Long Island : 'I had never felt myself particularly called into this special field of Christian labor [meaning the W. C. T. U.], so well occupied by so many faithful women of the land, especially in the village of Jamaica, partly because I was away from home so much, and therefore could not attend the meetings of the society regularly, and partly because I had fancied to myself that I had not much talent in the direction of this particular work. But by the urging of many of my very dear sisters connected with the society, I finally consented to do what I could to help on the work of "rescuing the perishing" around us.

"'I had never for one moment lost sight of the fearful ravages of strong drink among the people, and how the demon of rum threw his gluttonous length across the pathway of the Church. But I had so many other things to occupy my mind that I was innocently unconscious of my duty in this direction. I now see what a mistake I have made, and have repented in dust and ashes.

"'At one of our meetings in Beaver Street there came in a poor woman whose appearance from head to foot was repulsive to the last degree. Her clothing was shabby, her hair uncombed and disheveled, her face blotched and bloated, her eyes red and bleared, and her whole body trembling like an aspen leaf. I

talked with her about her soul, but was made sick by
the stench of her liquor-fumed breath. I told her
with all the persuasiveness of love which I could
command of her sorrowful end, and that "no drunk-
ard could enter the kingdom of heaven;" and then
I told her of the great love of Christ for sinners and
his almighty power to save the vilest of the vile, and
how ready the good sisters of this society were to help
her and pray for her and guide her trembling feet
into the path of peace. But my words to her and
my zeal for her salvation were repulsed by her saying, "What matters; I'm poor and despised any way,
and might as well be damned; who cares?' Then
the thought of my compassionate Lord came to me
with unwonted power, and I recovered myself from
this momentary repulse and seeming defeat, and said
to her, "As long as I live I will pray for you." Her
eye seemed to brighten a little at this, and I gained
some faith in her case by this momentary reviving of
hope in her breast. The meeting closed, and the poor
woman went her way again, as I feared, to her cups,
and from the dram-shop to her squalid hovel, and to
her confirmed debauchery. My faith faltered, but,
O, how I prayed for her poor soul that night, and the
Lord assured me that the "candlestick was *not yet*
removed out of its place." Try the case again was
the command from heaven.

" 'At our next meeting she came again, but her case seemed as hopeless as ever, and my words as useless as ever. I told her how I had prayed for her the night before, and how I had received impressions from the good Spirit in regard to her case; but my anxiety was met with only a half drunken smile of derision and contempt for my interest in her. As before, I assured her of my love and my purpose to pray for her still more. "*Nobody loves me*," was her heartless reply. This meeting closed, as before, with no visible sign of contrition, nor word of promise to reform.

" 'On my way home Satan said, "You are casting pearls before swine." Then I said, "This work of saving souls is the *Lord's work;* the work of pulling men into hell is the devil's work; I'll keep on the praying and the saving."

" ' At our next meeting the woman came again, this time somewhat improved in her personal appearance, and, as I thought, I saw a change in her moral condition—there was certainly an improvement in her breath—but she still trembled and was defiant. I said, "Do you pray for yourself? I am praying for you; will you not pray for yourself?" She said, "I wish I knew how to pray." I replied, "Repeat after me, 'God be merciful to me a sinner.'" She did so again and again. After a little the poor woman looked up into my face so imploringly, and said, "*Does any one care for me?*" Then came the supreme moment of my life. *Something*—the blessed Holy Spirit —said, "*Kiss her!*" How could I? Can I kiss those lips that have so long pressed the wine-cup and so long blasphemed the name of my adorable Lord? How can I do it? Then I said to myself, "My kiss may save a soul from death;" and then gathering up my spiritual courage (my natural courage was not enough for such a duty, for it was a duty) upon the one point of doing it for the dear Lord's sake, I bent over her and kissed her lips with as much faith as I had prayed in faith for her salvation the nights before. Immediately she burst into tears, and crying as if her heart would break, she said, "I see it now, I see it now; I will do better, I will live better. *You have kissed away my wretched life; you have kissed away my wretchedness.* Your kiss of love has brought me back to my better self again; the Lord has answered my prayers and saved my poor soul."'

"When Sister Weeden had reached this stage in her story there was not one in the meeting but was bathed in tears. I felt—all felt—what a going down into the valley of humility this was for her; but she took up the apparent repulsive cross and won a soul to Jesus. Then she told of her own joy that followed, of her happiness, as the glory of the Lord's sunshine—

a happiness divinely bestowed, and a happiness that sat and smiled.

"She had followed in the path of duty in meekness, charity, and love; she had seen the penitent's tear dried and a wounded heart bound up; a bruised spirit anointed with sympathy; a guilty soul forgiven, and virtue's feeble fire fanned to a flame; a soul for whom Christ died sitting in a light and holy place, and her joy was the joy of the Lord.

"'But my love for the poor woman was put to another test. At our next meeting this saved woman gave me an invitation to come and spend an afternoon with her and stay to tea. Then again grace triumphed. The invitation was accepted and the day fixed.

"At the appointed time there appeared at my yard gate what was once called a horse, but now it was poor, lame, and dejected, and needed only to be pushed over to be a fit subject for burial. And what shall I say of the harness? it was part leather, part rope, part cord, and part twine, and the whole put together in the most ungainly manner. And what of the wagon? True, there were four wheels to it, but no two alike, and the body was in the greatest tumble-down condition of any thing I ever saw in the shape of a wagon. But we got in, and off we started. During the whole of the journey she told me of her fallen life, of the change that had come to her home as well as to her own heart and

life, of her joy in the Lord, and not once did she
speak by way of apology of her traveling rig. We
finally reached her home. Every thing around on
the outside of the house and every thing inside showed
what intemperance would do for its poor victim.
But there appeared evidences on all sides of an effort
to fix up things a little; the yard was cleaned of old
rubbish, and the house was arranged on the inside
with as much care as possible under the circumstances.
The floor was without carpets; some of the chairs had
been broken, and now were hastily mended; the table
was worn and leafless. In fact, the whole outlook
was wearing the appearance of "improved poverty."
The meal she furnished was simple but neatly arranged,
and the redeemed and saved woman did her utmost to
make the visit pleasant and agreeable, and to us both
profitable. We talked about Jesus, we sang of Jesus,
we prayed to God in Jesus's name, and there was light
and joy in that humble home.

"'Dear sisters, let us gird on anew the armor of God,
"and go forth without the camp bearing his reproach
until evening."' Sister Nettie then sang:

> "'Down in the human heart,
> Crushed by the tempter,
> Feelings lie buried that grace can restore:
> Touched by a loving heart,
> Wakened by kindness,
> Chords that were broken will vibrate once more.'

" After the song she sat down amid the sobbings and shoutings of the congregation.

" How many people there are who are sighing for an opportunity of doing good, and yet fail to see the openings of a good providence where they might do many little things.

> " 'If we want a field of labor,
> We can find it anywhere.'

> " ARVINE C. BOWDISH.

" BROOKLYN, March 1, 1890."

CHAPTER XXVI.

Visits Danbury, Conn.—Services There.—Ocean Grove.—Wonderful Baptism.—Greenpoint Tabernacle.—Was it for Work?—"As I Knew Her."—Rev. S. A. Sands.

IT was during the summer of 1888 that we received a cordial invitation from the official members of the Methodist Episcopal church in Danbury, Conn., to supply their pulpit for a few weeks in the absence of their pastor.

It was on one of these visits we were accompanied by Nettie and her sister. After this visit there came out in the village paper the following :

" The temperance meeting held in Union Hall yesterday afternoon was fairly attended. The singing and prayer concluded, the assembly was addressed by the Rev. Francis C. Hill, from Long Island, after which his daughter, Mrs. Nettie Hill Weeden, followed with an earnest, loving appeal to the friends of the cause, after which her sister sang a solo, accompanied by the organ.

" The remarks uttered by Mrs. Weeden at this meeting should have been listened to by a crowded house, as they were full of earnest and eloquent thought, which every husband, wife, and child ought to have participated in.

"Sunday evening the Methodist Episcopal church was crowded ; chairs were placed in the side aisles, and yet a large number remained standing. Mrs. Weeden occupied the service by an earnest and loving exposition of the Scripture narrative of Jesus at Jacob's well, as found in the fourth chapter of John, dwelling mostly on the words of Jesus about the 'living water.' During this address she held the audience in deepest attention for more than half an hour. Many were bathed in tears and strong men were seen to sob as children.

"Seldom do strange people come among us and gain so rapid a hold on the people as the Rev. Mr. Hill and his daughters, and many will remember with lasting pleasure their presence and services."

Visit to Ocean Grove.

For many years the subject of this memorial desired to attend the annual meeting at this far-famed religious metropolis, but because of engagements and other reasons she had been prevented. This year, August, 1889, the way seemed providentially opened. In company with some dear friends she went. Upon her arrival there she entered at once into the spirit and enjoyment of the meeting. On Saturday a meeting was held in the Memorial Building; Nettie was invited to take charge of the meeting. During its progress she arose and began to relate her Christian experience. To the most of that large gathering, numbering, perhaps, a thousand persons, she was an entire stranger. Most of them had never heard or seen her before.

We have an account given by one who was present in the congregation:

"During the relation of her experience, which she did in her simple and loving manner, God began to pour out his Spirit upon the people. The scene was one of indescribable glory, bearing a striking resemblance to the day of Pentecost.

"As she stood upon the platform, lifted above the world, her face seemed lighted up as by an unearthly illumination, while there fell upon that large audience the baptism of the Spirit. Just now occurred a scene of strange interest. Some wept, some shouted, others arose from their seats and walked hurriedly to and fro, some laughed and waved their handkerchiefs. To one looking upon the scene from the outside it would appear as the greatest possible confusion, and some might have repeated what was charged upon the disciples more than eighteen hundred years ago: 'These men are drunk with new wine.' But to those within that charmed circle it was God coming near the peo-

15

ple, while a mighty wave of salvation rolled through
the camp of God's Israel. It was the cry of those
who had 'the mastery' through the blood of the
Lamb."

Such was the experience of that day at Ocean
Grove, a scene described by one as so wonderful and
unearthly as never to be forgotten as long as mind and
memory remain.

The next day, Saturday, she came by previous engagement to spend the Sabbath with us at the Greenpoint Tabernacle, Brooklyn. She spoke of the wondrous baptism she had received. We could see, because there yet lingered upon her countenance, some
of the glory she had received as she came down from
the mount of vision.

The next day being the Sabbath, she took a part
in the public services of the Tabernacle. Her address
to the Sabbath-school was simple, but in power. In
the afternoon she spoke to a large congregation for
thirty minutes or more from the words, "Unto her
was granted that she should be arrayed in fine linen,
clean and white." She appeared to have the largest
liberty and spoke as with the unction of the holy One.
It was truth sweetly presented, close and searchingly
applied by a bright sword that seemed to cut every
way.

We had heard her many times before, often with

delight, but never as on this occasion. As we sat in the congregation we looked upon her with wonder and amazement. The Holy Spirit was present, but unlike the scene described of two days before, there was no outward excitement, very little noise, save the suppressed utterance of those many baptized believers, while tears fell from eyes that seldom wept.

The many friends said: "God has anointed our dear Nettie for work and usefulness as never before." Some said : "She has come down from the Mount of Transfiguration, having been with Christ and seen his glory, and now as never before has received the enducement of power." That seemed to be the reasonable interpretation of this new gift received by her. How strange it appears! For other purposes than work in the Lord's earthly vineyard had she been thus anointed, for it was her last public service save one (of which we shall speak).

Like Moses, she was lifted to Nebo's height, and with strengthened vision was permitted to look out on scenes beyond before she was called to pass over. Who can tell what significance this blessed baptism had to work in regions beyond to which the Lord was soon to summon her? "Say ye, the Lord hath need of her." Who can say how or tell where?

Before we pass to the closing scenes of her life we desire to refer to those qualities of character that lifted

her above the ordinary level of society, that made her
one of Christ's "living epistles, known and read of all
men." It was her union and fellowship with God
—the "branch in the vine"—a living experience
thoroughly wrought and deeply rooted in every fiber
of her being. In its outward expression it flowed on
in beauty and strength as a river. It was fervent and
even demonstrative, yet not of a noisy, boisterous
kind.

During her first Christian years there were times
when an overflow of religious joy would find expression in laughter. At such times the Lord would
seem to put upon her the garment of joy and
praise, and for awhile she would be overcome with it,
like the psalmist, who said, "Then was our mouth
filled with laughter, and our tongue filled with singing."

A number of years before his death the Rev.
Dr. James Porter became acquainted with her. He
says: "I saw her at the Merrick Camp-meeting; it
was my first visit at that place. During a meeting
held in a large prayer-meeting tent my attention was
attracted to a young lady who appeared to be overcome with religious joy giving expression to her feelings by hearty laughter. I became much interested,
for I had witnessed such cases in the earlier years of
Methodism. I inquired who she was, and from that

time I formed an interesting acquaintance with her. I often heard her songs and testimonies. I saw in her one of God's dear saints, whose life and walk was a beautiful exhibit of the power of grace to cleanse from all sin, and I thoroughly believed in and admired her Christian character."

But these rhapsodies were only occasional. More generally her feelings found expression in a smile, with eyes suffused with tears. She never in public, and very seldom in private, spoke of her trials and conflicts. She did not think her Saviour was honored by such a recital. Hers it was to show the sunny side of religion, and yet no words of unbecoming levity were heard from her lips. To her, most emphatically, wisdom's ways were ways of pleasantness, and all her paths were peace.

With such an expression of feeling we are not to suppose her to have been without trials and sore conflicts, " whereof all are partakers." These she had, and sometimes of no ordinary character. She understood the meaning of those words, " Though now for a season, if need be, ye are in heaviness [not darkness] through manifold temptations : that the trial of your faith, being much more precious than of gold that perisheth, *though it be tried by fire.*" These trials of her faith were very severe, costing a struggle. Sometimes she would unbosom her heart to her dearest friends, but the outer circle would know but little of her conflicts. The outcome of these trials was to knit her soul more closely to her loving Burden-Bearer, and to yield to her the "peaceable fruits of righteousness."

An earnest Christ disciple was recently heard to say he would be glad to see one person who was fully a Christian.

To come up to his standard into every part of life, unto all its activities, Jesus Christ must enter and reign. We believe our sainted Nettie was one of that type. The Methodist Church was very dear to her, and to its doctrines and Discipline she was conscientiously loyal. But the voice of Jesus in her soul commanded her deepest love and obedience. "Let this mind be in you which was also in Christ Jesus," was her ideal. The Holy Spirit had implanted in her the "mind of Christ." There was nothing that so much delighted her as to see men and women saved—lifted heavenward. Works to her were a moral necessity. She believed and insisted that this was the purpose and object of her life. "We are his workmanship, created in Christ Jesus unto *good works.*" Works were not only a sign, but a seal of her "new creation."

The following is from Nettie's sister, concerning whom she had often said, "God gave me this dear one to take the place of my precious Anna Landon, who was early taken from me." It will be read with deepest interest, because it was the last meeting and public service she attended on earth, being the evening previous to her fatal illness :

" Friday evening, the twenty-first day of September, 1890, will always bring sad memories to those who on that evening met Nettie for the last time in a public meeting. Did the thought of this present itself to her as she walked down the familiar street and through the gate over the threshold of her home for the last time ? Ah ! who can tell ' what a day will bring forth ?' Human life is full of painful surprises. Little did those who were with her dream as she removed her wraps and gossamer and laid aside her over-shoes that she in so short time would lay aside her mortal garments and lie down in her last long sleep.

" The meeting to which allusion is made was of the Christian Endeavor Society connected with the Methodist Episcopal church, Jamaica. She had made preparation to make this meeting, if possible, of unusual interest, and had invited some members of her family to assist her by some special music.

" The meeting from the first assumed a most interesting character. The subject for the evening was ' a common-sense every-day service.' The leader, by a happy faculty she possessed, succeeded in bringing forth from nearly all present remarks and experiences bearing upon the subject. One of the remarks uttered by herself was this: ' Whatever I do I desire to do it in a thorough manner. If I am a housekeeper, I want to make the very best bread and have one of the neatest and best kept houses to be found.' This was not mere theory with her, as all who knew her could affirm; for she bestowed the same painstaking labor upon her home that she did in her more prominent public service; and this thought she strongly applied to Christian work. Near the close of the meeting she desired me, as I presided at the organ, to sing for her one of her favorite pieces, ' Guide me, O thou great Jehovah,' * and in a pleasant and familiar way called upon the audience to express their desire for the song by a vote, which was hearty and unanimous. So I sang it from memory just as I knew she would like it best, forgetting for the time myself and audience and only thinking of her. What strange realm of fancy it is where spirits blend, or where strong presentiments creep over the soul! At the close of the song there was a silence, in which the ticking of the clock only was heard, and which the leader broke by saying: ' Could I have my desire it would be to have that voice and song the last I should hear when I come to pass over the river.' Observing my emotion, as all were bathed in tears, she announced the closing hymn,

---

* From *Martha*, by Pattison.

which was followed by the pastor's benediction, and her last meeting on earth closed.

"I gently chided her for forcing me to lose my composure. Calling me by the familiar family name, she said: 'Doll, you would not like to have me leave you, would you?'

"As she passed down the aisle, exchanging greetings, a young friend and namesake, throwing her arms around her neck, said, with a voice choking with emotion: 'O, you are not going to leave us.' She replied: 'Not for three weeks yet,' referring to an engagement she had made to conduct religious work in Connecticut. 'But,' said the young lady, 'I have had a dream of you that saddens my heart and makes me fear you are to leave us soon for good.' Strange presentiment, so soon fulfilled! She did leave us, and as the breath of passing roses lingers, there yet remains a sweet perfume."

CHAPTER XXVII.

ON the morning of September 22, 1889, in the early train, there came to our home in Huntington a friend, bearing the intelligence of Nettie's illness. At five o'clock in the afternoon we were at her bedside. We found her prostrate and very ill indeed.

Early on that morning (Saturday) she had arisen apparently as well as usual. After attending to household duties she walked into the yard to enjoy the sweet air and sunshine. She was much interested in the growth of some young fruit-trees in the garden. As she paused to look at them she was seized with the fatal disease that ended in her death. She was able with difficulty to reach the house. When coming in she said to her sister, "Doll, I feel very bad." As her sister looked she saw at once that something serious had taken place. Her mouth was

HOUSE IN WHICH NETTIE DIED.

slightly drawn, while her countenance indicated an unnatural appearance. She walked to the kitchen to wash ; here she found she had lost the use of her left hand, and was obliged to lift it with the other. There was no mistaking the symptoms. Paralysis had fixed its leaden grasp upon her. A physician was summoned. When he came our worst fears were realized, as he declared such was the case. Her left side was paralyzed. Although helpless, she retained the use of her voice, and could speak distinctly and without difficulty. This remained until within a few hours of her death. This first attack seemed to yield to medical treatment, and gradually feeling and power were restored to her limbs. We were all encouraged, and hoped she would rally again. For this we earnestly prayed. We did not realize it possible that our precious one was to die. During the following week she gained strength. All through this her mind was calm and cheerful. She talked freely with her friends and sang and prayed. She was naturally timid, and shrank at the thought of death. As to what was beyond death she had no fears or distrust; but to her there had always been a dread of dying. Yet during all this illness, from first to last, she seemed to have entire victory over fear.

She said to us, "O, pa, I am wonderfully saved from fear." Frequently she talked about dying with the utmost composure. To her mother she said, "Ma, I would like to get well and do more for my Saviour, who has done so much for me. But if I should not I am all ready; I have no fears; I am saved. Ma, you and pa led me to the Saviour years ago. O, my dear ma, be faithful a little longer."

Brother H. C. McBride, her pastor, and his excellent wife called to see her. During their call she sang with them, and seemed to be wondrously lifted above the world, while her countenance beamed with heavenly illumination. Allusion was made to the doctrine and experience of entire sanctification. A feeling of sorrow seemed to affect the pastor's heart while he said, "So many are opposed to it." Nettie replied, "It is nothing strange nor new; it has ever been the case. O, Brother McBride, preach it fully and faithfully. God will help you and take care of the results. Souls will be fully saved."

Often to us she has spoken these words: "Don't fail, pa; don't be discouraged; preach a full salvation; it's what hungry souls need and are crying for."

One night she had a relapse. The family had retired, leaving only her mother and husband with her. Her strength seemed at once to leave her; a death-like paleness came over her face. We were summoned to her bedside; she was conscious but unable to speak.

We thought our dear child was about leaving us. But she rallied again; stimulants were used, and she so far recovered as to be able to speak, when she smilingly said, "O, ma, you thought I was going to leave you, did you not?"

"Yes," was the reply; "we thought you were about to go."

"But I had no fear," she said; "I felt it was all victory."

At another time she sang that beautiful hymn she had recently learned at Ocean Grove, "I've anchored my soul in the haven of rest." Looking to her husband she said, "What a blessed place to anchor." At one time she said to her husband, "Weedy, I have wanted a little home here that we could call our own. I shall not have it, but I shall have a mansion in heaven." At times her mind appeared to be almost entirely lost to this world, while things unseen seemed to fill her soul.

"Do you think," she asked her mother, "that Anna will know me?" alluding to her dear little sister, the companion of her childhood.

"Yes, my dear."

"Do you think Jesus will know me?" Of this there was no doubt, for in her soul there was a sweet whisper, "Yes."

"Do you suppose my name is written in heaven?

Yes," answering herself, "angels will speak it, and they will say, 'Here comes Nettie Hill Weeden, washed in the blood of the Lamb.'"

Her patience was perfect through all her illness. There were times when the pain she suffered was great, but not one word of complaint or murmur escaped her lips. When looking at her paralyzed arm and hand she smilingly said, "Pa, there will be no paralytics in heaven."

A short time before her illness she attended her class. The leader read at its opening of King Asa's zeal and consecration in cleansing the house of God. The thought came as an inspiration. The leader said, "We two will make a clean sweep for God." The spirit and testimony of the meeting followed in the same line.

In this her last illness, while lying on a bed of suffering, with a part of her body paralyzed, she called for pencil and paper, and wrote the following with this as its heading:

"A CLEAN SWEEP."

"A CLEAN SWEEP OF ALL FOR HEAVEN;
IT WILL PAY A SWEET RETURN.

"A clean sweep—from worldlyhonor
This will be—must be, entire;
For the two, like fire and water,
One must live and one expire.

" A clean sweep—in Christian service
  To fling those pillars down
Of pride, and fear, and self-devotion,
  To work for Christ, and him alone.

"A clean sweep—of all our talents,
  Voices rough and language hard;
They will shine for God most brilliant
  When his light on them is turn'd.

" A clean sweep—for God and glory;
  Every idol, every love
Shall be sanctified and holy,
  Fitted for the home above.

" A clean sweep—from worldly passion,
  Faithful now our God to prove;
Pride and pomp and worldly fashion,
  Captives slain by holy love.

"A clean sweep—from social follies
  That take sweetness from the life;
All for God, Holy of Holies,
  End of care, end of strife.

"On this bed of pain and suffering
  I to Christ surrender all;
'Tis at best an humble offering,
  Yet 'tis loved, for it's the whole.
              " NETTIE HILL WEEDEN."

On Sunday, the 29th, she so far recovered her strength as to get up and walk out in the dining-room, and with her husband sit down to the table. Eating a little, she returned, and, lying down on a lounge, fell into a quiet slumber for an hour, when, upon awakening, another and severer shock came. To the family this was the harbinger of death! It now became evident her end was drawing near. Still it was the will of God that her mind should be clear, and that she should be able to converse a little with the family. Her feet were already in the chilling waters of death. We asked her, "My dear, have you had peace to-day?" We had been absent a few hours. She replied:

"O, yes; my peace has been as a river." And then added, "O, how sweetly I am kept—kept from fear."

This she repeated many times. During the last night we watched by her side. Her limbs were quiet and composed; her last song had been sung; her tongue was no more to give utterance to words, so often spoken to cheer our hearts and to bless hundreds. With eyes closed upon friends, never to open them again in this world, she was now going down into the valley. Her labored breathing gave indications that death was nigh.

Dear reader, did you ever watch by the dying bed of one you dearly loved, as you saw the surging waves roll higher and yet higher, while each beating pulse but more surely marked the waning hours of mortal strife? If so, you may understand our experience of that last night. It was sad to see our precious one pass down into the shadows.

We could not tell of nor measure her bodily sufferings. Whatever they were we would have gladly shared them with her; but the connecting earthly link between us was broken. In our deep, unutterable sorrow we cried to God for help. Upon our knees we prayed, "O, Master, if she cannot speak do thou speak. Out of this tempest throw a ray of light to our agonized and bleeding hearts." And he did speak! We opened our little pocket Testament and read, as the voice of God: "They shall hunger no more, neither thirst any more; neither shall the sun light on them, nor any heat. For the Lamb which is in the midst of the throne shall feed them, and shall lead them unto living fountains of waters: and God shall wipe away all tears from their eyes."

A thousand times we had read these words before, and by them sought to comfort other hearts that sorrowed; but never until that night had their wonderful depth and meaning been made known to us. With this new revelation there came a flood of light, and peace filled the dying chamber. "Privileged above the common walks of virtuous life, quite on the verge of heaven." With a chastened yet overflowing heart we praised the Lord. The night had passed! One breath longer and deeper, as if tired of the strife,

16

then gently falling asleep as a weary child upon its mother's bosom. As the rising sun touched with rosy finger the eastern sky the messenger angel called her softly, saying, " COME," when without a struggle or a groan she was not, for God had taken her. The descending chariot "swung low," and she passed the pearly gates to take HER "CROWN," studded with " STARS," and her " SPOTLESS ROBE."

AND IT WAS MORNING!

" God's singer! In a land
Of alien thought and language thou didst sing
The songs of Zion. Now before thy King,
Blest singer, thou dost stand.

" Thine earthly singing o'er—
Thy singing sweet and strong and glad and wise—
Thou art among the choir of Paradise
A singer evermore ! "

CHAPTER XXVIII.

Carried to the Church.—White Casket.—Prophetic Dream Fulfilled.—" Deliverance has Come."—Services.—Speakers : Rev. B. M. Adams, Rev. William T. Pray, Rev. H. C. McBride.—Taken to Riverhead.—Laid to Rest beside " Precious Anna " and Kindred.—Farewell.—A Sister's Tribute.

ON Friday afternoon we took all that was mortal of our dear one to the church, where in front of the altar she was placed, lying in a white casket, with clasped hands and pale face, yet beautiful in death.

That was only the house of clay. It was all left to us of the earthly form. Out from that tabernacle had gone the spirit that had occupied it. Her prophetic "dream" had been fulfilled. She, the *real one*, had doubtless paused on the " threshold of limitless life " to take a view of the house she was leaving behind until they should meet again, as meet they will. There were but few of the vestments of death. She appeared as if clad in bridal robes.

During her life she had often sung, " Deliverance will come," and had charged her friends, " When I am gone I desire you to write on my monument,

" Deliverance has Come."

A large number of ministers were present, many of them taking a part in the services. The principal speakers were: Rev. B. M. Adams, Presiding Elder of the District; Rev. William T. Pray, her former pastor; and Rev. H. C. McBride, her pastor at the time of her death. From these men of God, who had known her "purpose and manner of life," there were spoken words of sweetest consolation.

With stricken hearts, amid tears, there ascended prayers to Him whose heart is ever touched with sympathy for human sorrow, that her mantle might fall upon the bereaved home and church. There were thanksgivings because of her labors and holy triumph.

In front of the altar, watched by loving ones, she remained through the night. The next morning, with mourning friends, she was taken to Riverhead and laid in the family plot in the beautiful cemetery by the side of her "precious sister," surrounded by the graves of departed ones of the family, where in due time father and mother, with those she loved so much, will take their places until the dawn of that bright morning when death shall be despoiled and broken links once more united. "Even so, Lord Jesus, come quickly."

> "Farewell! to the world;
> My task is o'er, my work is done,
> And spent the weary day;

I've fought the fight, the battle's won,
And I must haste away;
Henceforth there is laid up for me
A ' crown ' through all eternity.

" A crown by hands eternal wove,
Meet for a child of God,
Gemmed with jewels of his love,
And purchased with his blood,
Which human hands could ne'er have wrought.

" Farewell the cross 'neath which
I've watched and fought so long,
And welcome now the harp and song
That 'wait me where I go;
Yet O! that cross must still be dear,
Though borne by many a sorrow here.

" And oft throughout eternity,
'Mid all that's bright and best,
Its victory my joy shall be,
And I will love it best;
For 'twas through Him who died thereon
My fight was fought, my battle won."

Opposite page 246 is a picture of Nettie's grave,
by the side of which is seen the tomb of " Little Anna
Landon." In the adjoining plot in the rear the tall
spire marks the spot where lie the remains of her grandfather and grandmother. On the left is seen the monument of her Uncle George. On the right is the large
granite shaft beneath which rest the remains of her
Uncle William. Directly on the right, though unseen,
repose all that is mortal of her Aunt Julia and her

husband, S. J. Vail, upon whose monument is inscribed his name and age, with this touching addition :

"THE AUTHOR OF

'SCATTER SEEDS OF KINDNESS'

AND

'GATES AJAR.'"

"There are no monuments so interesting in this world as the tombs of men, especially those of our kindred."

"This is the last of earth."

"Thy dead men shall live, together with my dead body shall they arise. Awake and sing, ye that dwell in dust: for thy dew shall be as the dew of herbs, and the earth shall cast forth her dead."

"Thou art gone to the grave; but we will not deplore thee
    Whose God was thy ransom, thy guardian, and guide;
    He gave thee, he took thee, and he will restore thee,
    And death has no sting, for the Saviour hath died."

The following account of the funeral services is from the *Brooklyn Daily Times :*

"MRS. WEEDEN LAID AT REST.

"*Funeral service at the Jamaica Methodist Episcopal Church.— An impressive ceremony attended by an immense gathering.— The clergymen participating, the flowers and the music.—A brief life sketch.*

"The Methodist Episcopal Church, Jamaica, was filled to the doors yesterday afternoon with the sor-

RIVERHEAD, LONG ISLAND.

rowing friends of the late Mrs. Nettie Hill Weeden, the well-known evangelist, who died at her home in that village on Wednesday morning last. They came from all quarters, and the village main street was crowded with strangers for an hour before the service began. The remains reposed in a white casket covered with floral emblems in front of the altar; and as the choir sang " I Heard a Voice from Heaven" the scene was very impressive. The service was conducted by the Rev. H. C. McBride, pastor of the church, assisted by the Rev. B. M. Adams, Presiding Elder; the Rev. Dr. A. C. Bowdish, of St. Paul's Church, Brooklyn; and the Rev. William T. Pray, the former pastor, now of Cypress Hills. There were also present the Rev. J. V. Saunders, of Sheepshead Bay; the Rev. W. Gillies, of Lawrence; the Rev. Calvin E. Ford, of Huntington; the Rev. Edward Warriner, of Rockville Center; the Rev. John Brien, of Springfield; the Rev. L. Richardson, of New York, and Evangelist Thomas Elgar, of Jamaica. Addresses were made by Presiding Elder Adams, the Rev. William T. Pray, and the Rev. H. C. McBride. The two former spoke in eulogistic terms of her life and character as a promoter of the religion of Christ, and her evangelistic labors generally. Mr. McBride, the deceased lady's pastor, referred in feeling terms to her sickness and death, dwelling upon her great fortitude and resignation. 'Naturally timid,' said Mr. McBride, 'and shrinking at the thought of death, there was something that always was with her that gave her courage. During all her illness from the first she had an entire victory. She said to her father, "I am wonderfully saved from fear," and while the family were alarmed she remained calm.'

"The musical selections by the choir included Mrs. Weeden's favorite hymn, 'Haven of Rest,' and the hymn 'Meet Me There.' By request of the family Mrs. McBride, the pastor's wife, sang the solo, 'Gathering Home,' rendering it with thrilling effect. The flowers were rich and magnificent. The Society of Christian Endeavor, of which the late evangelist was a member, sent an anchor, and Mr. John C. Acker's class, with which she was connected, a beautiful basket and cross. The officers, teachers, and scholars of the Jamaica, South, Sunday-school attended in a body, carrying in their hands bouquets of flowers. As they passed around to view the body at the close of the service each one laid his or her bouquet on the casket, the aggregate making a beautiful floral mound.

"The pall-bearers were L. M. Wood, Alfred H. Beers, John C. Acker, Thomas Clary, Isaac B. Remsen, and John Selover. The body remained in the church all night, six ladies and six gentlemen acting as watchers. This morning it was taken to Riverhead, where it was interred in the family plot.

"With the death of Mrs. Weeden there passes away one of the best-known and best-loved women that ever lived on Long Island. In her the Christian character attained its full development, and her life, devoted to the lifting up of others, presents a beautiful picture of love and devotion. Whoever was privileged to enjoy her society realized the breadth and depth of her character, and those to whom she ministered were at once brought under the influence of her personal magnetism. As an evangelist she was known from one end of Long Island to the other, as well as in New York and Brooklyn ; and multitudes to-day who have listened to her winning and persuasive eloquence and have been charmed by her presence are sorrowing at her loss.

"Mrs. Weeden was born in Hempstead forty-six years ago. Her father, the Rev. Francis C. Hill, and mother and husband, Mr. David J. Weeden, survive her. Her religious experience began at the Carlton Avenue Church, Brooklyn, twenty five years ago, when she became strongly impressed with a desire to lead others in the path she had chosen, and ultimately became an evangelist, having derived her training chiefly from her father. For ten years preceding her death she gave herself to evangelistic labor, achieving great success wherever she went, and being in constant demand. She labored in New York and Brooklyn, and at many points on Long Island ; among them being Sayville, Setauket, Stony Brook, Amityville, and Jamaica, South. She was a prominent figure at camp-meetings, the last she attended being that at Ocean Grove, N. J. At Merrick for many years she had charge of the children's meetings, a service in which she took a special delight. She was looking forward to an enlarged field of labor when she was stricken down with the disease which carried her off. Her cheery words and pleasant manner will be sadly missed."

The following were words, in part, spoken at the funeral by the Rev. B. M. Adams, Presiding Elder of the Brooklyn District :

". . . The darkness and sorrow are out of this funeral. In truth and gladness we can say,

> " 'Our sister the haven hath gained,
> Outstripping the wind and the tide.'

"It is a time for congratulations and praise. She has won the victory ! The white blood-washed soul has mounted the skies, and passed into the presence of her King and Saviour.

"She gave herself unreservedly to the great Head of the Church militant, and having served her probationship creditably to herself and profitably to the children of men, she has been received into full and eternal membership in the Church triumphant.

"What joy, what congratulations there must be on account of her arrival. What blessed recognitions by those in the heavenly assembly who are there through her instrumentality. What eager interest the angels must manifest and, blessed be God how pleased Jesus must be to have her with him.

"At funerals there is a tendency to over-estimate those whom we admire and love, and certainly it would be out of harmony with the tastes and modest bearing of our departed sister to claim for her the highest talent. It may be there are many Methodist women on Long Island who were her superiors. But we do say, she was on fire with the love of Jesus—a blazing heart that made her a power wherever she went.

"No woman in Long Island Methodism has been her peer for the last fifty years, since the great baptism came upon her. Since years ago she has been the one woman evangelist whom every body loved and welcomed at camp-meetings, churches, and firesides. Hundreds have been saved through her word.

"While she has been a faithful and true wife in her home, and a loving sister and friend in the family circle, the fact that she was a ministering spirit to her father in his work is deserving of more notice and emphasis than we have time on this occasion to give. He knows what she has been to him in his ministry, and what valuable assistance she has rendered. Perhaps at this period of his life he has desired her companionship, in her sweet songs, her spiritual conversation, and fervent prayers. But he doubtless submits to the Master's will and call, considering that she has been invited into the heavenly choir to do better service even than she did here.

"It was a beautiful thought to have this casket white. It is suggestive of the past, the present, and the future, as relating to Nettie Hill Weeden.

"Let the women of this congregation who knew and loved this pure and consecrated woman, as they come to see the empty clay, lay their hands on the white casket and give themselves to Nettie Weeden's God, to take up her work and multiply it until Long Island shall be filled with fire-baptized workers, and her work be carried on to wider victory."

A SISTER'S TRIBUTE.

"A pebble is cast into the calm waters of the lake; the circles widen until it is beyond the power of vision to follow them as their tiny wavelets lose themselves in some sheltered nook far up among the reeds and rushes. We may not trace their ripples to the hidden shores, nor count them as they follow one by one in distinct and perfect curves. Yet they continue on and on in regular succession, until the last one breaks upon the shore.

"Thus it is with human life. Its influence—who can fix its measure or set its boundaries?

"When once a loving spirit has made its impress and fixed its seal in this life, and passed to its native realm beyond, shall that influence cease and become lost? or shall it continue to affect human lives, to widen until the farther shores of eternity only can measure its extent? I write thus of my dear sister's life and character. She started ripples on the ocean of life that have for years been enlarging, reaching out in manifold directions.

"These were not less impressive or valuable to those who were nearest her. Within the limited circle of her home, where she was more fully known, was the wand of her magical influence felt. Her nature and character were such that no one could be long within their reach without feeling their potent influence. Naturally she was possessed of a lively and vivacious temperament, which carried the very essence of sunshine with her. It is true, like others of a similar nature, her sky was sometimes overcast: but it was never more than a passing cloud that the bursting sunshine would quickly chase away.

"Forming one of that charmed home circle, I can but record devout thanksgiving to my heavenly

Father, who gave me such a loving and devoted sister. Such she ever was to me from earliest infancy until the hour when 'the silent boatmen with muffled oar carried her spirit over the river.'

"My first recollections of this sainted sister present her as being just in the flower of young womanhood, occupied with her home and social duties, moving about in Christian work, and much engrossed in her musical studies, and devotedly fond of 'my little sister.' To me in my childhood and youth she imparted instruction and guidance in the way of life, and through those years was my musical instructor. These were sources of rarest pleasure shared alike by teacher and pupil. As mature years brought increased sedateness to one, they seemed never to dispel or diminish the winsome simplicity of the other. Hence the relationship was but a symbol of a congenial and delightful companionship which was continued, growing as the years have passed.

"It is not necessary to say *she is missed*, or that when the light of her presence went out it left a darkness and a void that time will never fill. Upon my heart and life her sisterly love and influence will never be measured. Nor did they cease with her life; but like the widening ripples they will continue until time shall give place to eternity.

"FRANCES E. HILL JOHNSON.

O'er the River.

F. E. H. J.

FRANCES E. HILL JOHNSON,
Dedicated to my Sister.

1. Tender mem'ries throng around us While we walk this vale of tears;
Waft - ed mel - o - dies surround us From the vanished days and years.

CHORUS.

On - ly just a-cross the riv - er, O'er the rapid flowing tide;
There u - nit - ed, we shall ev - er In our Father's Home abide.

2 Shall we find the links united
That were severed here in pain;
Flow'rs of love that here were blight-
Fadeless there to bloom again? [ed,

3 Shall we meet them at the Portal
Of the Palace of the King,
Robed in spotless white immortal,
Will they for our welcome sing?

4 Shall we know the tender greeting
That was ours in days of yore,
Will there be a joyous meeting
Over on the other shore!

5 One by one they went before us;
One by one we follow on,
Till united in a chorus,
We will sing—"The parting's done."

The following sketch is from the pen of the Rev. I. Simmons:

"TRANSLATED: HOW WE SHALL MISS HER.

"Mrs. Nettie Hill Weeden, daughter of Rev. Francis C. Hill, of the New York East Conference, died in Jamaica, L. I., October 2, 1889. She was born in Hempstead, L. I., February 15, 1844. She was converted in Brooklyn, a young lady of nineteen, and quickly developed into a life of faith and usefulness. Her conviction was so pungent as to deprive her of eating and sleep, and was followed by the rapture that kept the bells of heaven ringing in her soul for all her years. She was free from doubt, never looked reluctantly to the Goshen she had left, never slid back into an easy-going religion.

"In July, 1870, at the Oakington National Camp-meeting, she bowed before the Lord, seeking the blessing of entire sanctification. As clear as her conversion came the cleansing grace, to which in glowing terms and with shining face she loved to revert. Her life and labors bore testimony to the joyous truth. As an evangelist she wrought with holy skill, teaching and persuading under the unction of the holy One, and many at camp-meetings and in the churches by her side entered into the perfect rest. She was gentleness embodied, though courageous and fearless in declaring her experience of perfect love. I have heard her at times when the glory of the Lord shone in her countenance and a holy awe impressed me.

"Last August she received a wonderful baptism at Ocean Grove. It enriched and sweetened her life for the translation which was soon to follow. She was ready for service or sacrifice, and while preparing to enter the fall and winter campaign for Christ he announced his will that she should enter on higher service in his spiritual kingdom, and without a murmur she assented. And a great multitude join with the bereaved husband and afflicted parents and loved ones in their deep sorrow. Yet while the crowned servants are missed here, we bless God for the inspiration of their holy lives. She lived holy. She breathed the atmosphere of holiness. Under its potent sanctions she led many souls to conversion and the fount of cleansing. She could have sat in the pew and glided along the easier ways of church life as many others are satisfied to do; but her holy soul would not permit. All for Jesus means work, sacrifice, counting all service delight, if so be his glory abounds. Thank God for such saints! We watch their white light flashing out in the darkness of surrounding sinfulness, and we praise him. We remember their trials and patient endurance for the sake of souls, and we take courage to do our own work

17

better. We ask, What are their resources? and renew
our consecrations as the answer comes. Theirs is the
New Testament standard of piety. The men and
women who are to be the Lord's efficient helpers in
saving this world are those who are filled with his
spirit. Such an one, gentle, strong in faith, winsome
in manners, taught in the Scriptures, abundant in
sanctified common sense, walking consistently in the
light of perfect love, and faithfully turning many to
righteousness, was Mrs. Nettie Hill Weeden."

The following is from the Rev. S. A. Sands:

"As I Knew Her.

"I became acquainted with Sister Nettie Hill
Weeden at Merrick Camp-meeting full twenty years
ago. Her life then was 'all for Jesus.' Her testimony was always clear, her faith in the promises of
God was strong, her prayers were often of the 'I-will-
not-let-thee-go' kind.

"She was always at home among the children
and young people, who greeted her as a Christian
friend and leader, and whether they were young or
old, she was delighted to point to them the way and
help the seeking ones to her Jesus. But her soul never
seemed more in its native element than when among
those who were enjoying the blessing of heart-purity
or were seeking to enter that blessed state, and she

would be among the first to sing, 'Praise God, from whom all blessings flow.' Many has this saint helped over the Jordan into the Canaan of perfect rest.

" We never noticed but one change—namely, deeper and deeper, higher and higher, broader and broader, more and more of the wonderful love of Jesus shining through her life.

> " ' Servant of God, well done,
> Thy glorious warfare's past;
> The battle's fought, the victory's won,
> And thou art crowned at last.'

"North Woodbury, Conn., October 18, 1890."

We Watched Her.

> We watched her breathing through the night,
> Her breathing soft and slow,
> As in her breast the wave of life
> Kept waving to and fro.

> So silently we seemed to speak,
> So slowly moved about,
> As we lent her half our powers
> To eke her living out.

> Our weary hopes belied our fears,
> Our fears our hopes belied;
> We thought her dying when she slept
> And sleeping when she died.

> For when the morn came, dim and sad,
> And chill with early showers,
> Her quiet eyelids closed; she had
> Another morn than ours.

The following letter is from Rev. William Ross, with whom she labored at Lawrence, L. I.:

"New Rochelle, December 17, 1889.

"My Dear Brother Hill : Your note of November 27 was duly received. It ought to have been answered sooner, but I have been a little at a loss how to put my thoughts.

"Your dear Nettie was a most beautiful character ; sweet, gentle, loveable, all that one could look for in this crooked world. I think, too, she was called of God to the work she was engaged in. But as the blessed Master himself failed sometimes, through the unbelief of the people, so Nettie failed at Lawrence. Notwithstanding, she left a most hallowed impression. Every one felt and acknowledged the purity, the strength, and beauty of her character. They willingly, and even lovingly, testified to the high tone of her piety and the holiness of her walk and conversation.

*   *   *   *   *   *

"How mysterious are the ways of God. Why should Nettie be called away, when the work is so great and the (holy) laborers are so few ? I am sometimes perplexed by these questions. I deeply sympathize with you, my dear brother, in your great loss and in the great loss the churches have sustained in her removal. May God Almighty bless and sustain

you and yours. I am sorry I cannot give you something worthy of publication. Most gladly would I con-
tribute to the perpetuation of the memory of so good
a woman as Nettie Hill Weeden if I had the ability.
I greatly esteemed her. She was so gentle, so modest,
so unassuming, and yet so firm, so composed in the
great work God had given her to do. Heaven will
be sweeter to meet her there. God bless you all!

"Your brother in Christ,

"WILLIAM ROSS."

The following loving testimonial comes from the
Rev. John Parker, of the New York East Conference:

"321 East 50th Street, New York,
"November 20, 1890.

"*Rev. F. C. Hill:*

"DEAR BROTHER HILL: Yes, I knew your beloved
Nettie. When I was pastor at Jamaica she spent
two weeks with us in evangelistic work. The people
among whom, in her earlier beautiful life, she spent
the years of your pastorate there received her with
joy. She had their hearts, and held them by her devout simplicity and transparent sincerity. She helped
us to win for Christ twenty souls during her stay.
But she especially won the deeper esteem of all our
people, some of whom until then had been strangers
to her.

"If God's most wonderful and costly contribution to this world is a saintly life, and if, in his estimation, it is worth all it costs, then the life of Nettie, I doubt not, largely realized his ideal. Weighed in the balances, through the grace that so fully saved her, she was not found wanting. This was not her opinion of herself, but ours. I believe, also, it was His.

"Hers was a modest but luminous piety that rose heavenward on wings of song, until nearing the gates of day, they closed upon her and refused her return.

"She made us wish our lives divine;
We saw in her His image shine;
She taught us by his love to sing,
And how to soar on eagle's wing

"She fanned our joys with breath of praise,
Inflamed our zeal through earnest days;
She tired not in his service here,
Impatient to be with him there.

"Dear soul of song, made white through blood,
Most meet for thee to go to God;
No wonder now that he should call,
And thou shouldst hear and see it all.

"Too late for tears, but not for trust;
We can be holy, can and must;
Like thee, like him, fill earth with joy,
And share at last thy blest employ.

"Dear brother, accept this humble tribute.

"Yours with esteem—in Him,

"JOHN PARKER."

The following letter was received from Rev. I. Simmons, now stationed at Mount Vernon, N. Y. Until recently he had been the Presiding Elder upon the Brooklyn District, within which district Nettie resided. It is a consolatory communication to a bereaved home, as also a loving tribute to the translated one:

"56 West 2d St., Mt. Vernon, N. Y., {
"October 4, 1889. }

"*Rev. F. C. Hill:*

"Dearly Beloved Brother: I was shocked in reading in the paper that Nettie had gone. Not knowing any thing of her sickness, it was like the bursting of a storm from a clear sky. She was a blessed woman. Her life was so transparent and beautiful. I was at the National Camp-meeting at Oakington, Md., when she received the baptism of the Holy Ghost.

"I have occasionally since been with her in various parts of the field, more especially at several camp-meetings at Merrick. God was always with her, and many are the souls she has helped into the kingdom. Her record is glorious! I am very sorry I could not be with you, and say some comforting words to you and to Sister Hill and Brother Weeden. But the telegram came too late for me to make arrangements so that I could leave here on the 10:51, the last train that would enable me to reach Jamaica.

"God bless you and comfort you both, and please extend to Brother Weeden my sincere commiseration. We have told many weeping ones the way to comfort; we have whispered to them of the sympathizing Jesus.

"O, may he now draw preciously near to you and pour his peaceful balm into your spirits. Mrs. Simmons wishes me to express to you her sympathy and condolence.   Yours very truly,

"I. Simmons."

The following letter was received soon after her death by her husband:

"Commack, October 16, 1889.

"My Dear Brother Weeden: I desire to express to you the deep feelings of my people and of my own heart. We are touched with a deep sympathy for you in your bereavement.

"I preached a memorial sermon last Sabbath both at Commack and at Dix Hills. Could you have seen the sorrow and felt the sympathy, it would have alleviated your grief. The affection which the Dix Hills people manifested was very affecting. As I referred to her holy life and great spiritual influence in song, prayer, and testimony, my people felt they had been bereaved. Why? Eternity only will reveal the far-reaching results of her labors. It has been your joy and honor to have had such a companion.

"The churches have been moved and blessed, and sinners converted and believers enabled to see the need and blessedness of a pure heart from the experience and scriptural presentation of the glorious doctrine. She was helpful to me. Her shining face and persuasive manner lives on. 'She being dead, yet speaketh.'

"The Lord bless and comfort you, dear brother, and preserve you until when

> "'The morn those angel faces smile
> Which we have loved so long
> And lost awhile.'

"Praying for you, I am yours very truly,

"W. DALZIEL."

The following letter comes from a young Christian man, a local preacher now preparing for the ministry, a student in Drew Theological Seminary. It is addressed, as the former letter, to the bereaved husband:

"MADISON, N. J., October 5, 1889.

"DEAR BROTHER WEEDEN: In this hour of your great affliction I must add, if possible, a few words of condolence in the great loss you have sustained in the death of your wife, and a few words as to her pure and exalted character. When I learned of her death it came as a great shock to me and tears filled my eyes. I cannot realize that Sister Weeden is no longer mortal, but immortal; no more earthly, but heavenly.

"No one knows but our families what an interest she always took in me, and none can over-estimate her value and help to me. Under her exhortation, in March, 1879, I first felt that I was a sinner, and through her persistent faith and encouragement I was led into the fountain of cleansing in August, 1886. After that feeling I was called to preach, which call followed me for years. When I told her of the exercises of my heart, she seemed to be overjoyed. She bade me be of good courage and go forward. During the later years her interest in me suffered no abatement. It could not have been greater if I had been her brother by blood. In the loss of such a saintly friend I am greatly afflicted. I bless and praise the Lord that I ever formed an acquaintance with her. I feel I am a much better man on that account. . . .

"God bless you, my dear brother. How bright and near heaven must be to you. Truly, another precious link binds you to the heavenly shore; another precious glorified form is beckoning you to higher attainments in spiritual life. By this sudden call I think I shall live closer to my Lord than ever before.

"Do give my kindest, prayerful sympathy to all the family, especially to dear Brother Hill and wife. May divine grace sustain you all. Amen.

"Your brother,

"HENRY C. WHITNEY."

"One less at home !
The charmed circle broken ; a dear face
Missed day by day from its accustomed place,
But *cleansed* and *perfected* by grace,
One more in heaven !

"One less at home !
One voice of welcome hushed, and evermore.
One farewell word unspoken ; on the shore
Where parting comes not one soul landed more.
One more in heaven !

"One more in heaven !
Another thought to brighten cloudy days,
Another theme for thankfulness and praise,
Another link on high our souls to raise
To home and heaven."

The following beautiful tribute comes from Rev.
William Pray, her pastor for three years in Jamaica,
L. I.

" ' The many tides of ocean
Are one vast tidal wave,
That sweeps in landward motion
Alike to coast and cave;
And life from Christ outflowing
Is one wave evermore,
To earth's dark caverns going,
Or heaven's bright pearly shore.'

"In vacation time, during student life, one bright
summer day, the privilege of attending camp-meeting
at Merrick, L. I., afforded an opportunity to look
upon an illumined face and to hear a pathetic voice ;

and, as in a portrait, sometimes, there are eyes which look upon us wherever we may stand, so, likewise, that face and voice could never be forgotten by any who engaged in the services of that day. That face appears before us yet, and that voice we remember still.

"In after years it was a delight and an honor to become the pastor, in Jamaica, L. I., of Nettie Hill Weeden, whose glowing words touched so many hearts on the memorable occasion at the camp-ground. From the stand-point of a pastorate of three years a few observations can be made. The presence of such a worker was quite an acquisition to the church. She was a good listener, and her responsive and express-ive countenance encouraged the preacher. Occasion-ally she occupied a portion of the time allotted to the public service on the Sabbath in giving a Bible-read-ing or an address upon some scriptural theme, with profit and delight to the congregation. Perhaps the most enjoyable exercise to herself, as well as to those who listened, was in the Sunday evening prayer-service, after the sermon by the pastor, when, with-out any special preparation, excepting the revolving in her mind of a few thoughts that had occurred to her during the meeting, she would arise, either volun-tarily or upon invitation, and with wonderful power deliver an address which carried with it the tokens of inspiration. It should be said, however, that she was familiar with the Scriptures and knew much about God, and, moreover, knew God; so that these were not times of mere venture to talk against time, nor of hap-hazard incoherent ranting. It ought to be said that she admitted her times of depression and felt fettered while speaking, but it can be safely claimed that, as a rule, she was a good illustration of the Master's declaration, 'Every scribe which is instructed unto the kingdom of heaven is like unto a man that is an householder, which bringeth forth out of his treasure things new and old.' When she entered the room where the prayer or class-meeting was held the leader always felt strengthened and the success of the meeting was assured, for she knew how to talk with God, she was ready with her testimony, and she sang appropriately and well; indeed, in her exercises Paul's expression was interpreted, 'I will pray with the spirit, and I will pray with the understanding also; I will sing with the spirit, and I will sing with the understanding also.'

"In regard to her own religious experience, she was firm and unflinching in her testimony that she had 'entered the valley of blessing,' and 'the blood of Jesus Christ cleanseth from all sin.' She courageously and fearlessly presented the Gospel of full salvation. From her position there was no deviation, saving that

she became increasingly intense in her advocacy of
the glorious truth and blessing; and in manner and
testimony evinced the spirit of Luther, who said,
' Here I stand ; I cannot do otherwise; God help me !
Amen.' And yet Sister Weeden was a modest
saint. Too much so at times. She was retiring and
avoided publicity as much as possible. Once in
awhile stood in the background, and so was passed by
unintentionally; and no doubt the tempter took advantage and her sensitiveness was tested. She courted
no compliments, and gave no ear to flattery. A
unique trait of character was detected in her as she
would be seen taking some pains to speak to some one
of the lowly of the earth who had been scarcely
noticed by others. She possessed ability, tact, and
grace. She was recognized by intelligent and cultured
people, and all classes regarded her with respect and
confidence. Her warm attachment toward her family
connections was noticeable. Her fondness for her
father as a minister of the Gospel was very apparent.
In her public remarks she frequently alluded to him,
and when he was present she was delighted.

" A few months ago, when a precious little girl in
the village was on the borders of the land of life
and immortality, she rejoiced at the prospect of seeing and knowing Mrs. Weeden. In a few hours the
bright anticipation was followed by a glorious reali-

zation. Similar feelings and prospects make heaven more desirable to all who have known Nettie Hill Weeden."

REST!

" Beautiful toiler, thy work is done;
Beautiful soul into glory gone,
Beautiful life with its crown now won,
    God giveth thee rest!
Rest from all sorrows and watchings and fears,
Rest from all possible sighing and tears,
Rest through God's wonderful years,
    At home with the blest.

"Beautiful spirit, free from all stain,
Ours the headache, the sorrow and pain,
Thine is the glory and infinite gain;
    Thy slumber is sweet.
Peace on thy brow, and the eyelids so calm;
Peace in the heart 'neath the white folded palm;
Peace dropping down, like a wondrous balm,
    From the head to the feet.

" 'It was so sudden!' our white lips said;
How we shall miss her, the beautiful dead.
Who take the place of the precious one fled?
    But God knoweth best.
We know he watches the sparrows that fall,
Hears the sad cry of the grieved hearts that call;
Friends, husband, parents—he loveth them all.
    We can trust for the rest."

Thou Art not Gone.

" Thou art not gone, though thy sleeping dust
  Is low in the silent grave,
And thy spirit is taken to realms of light
  By Him who died to save.

" For still thy sweet face and placid look
  Are present before our eye;
As long as we live thy form must live
  In our fondest memory.

" And yet the sound of thy loving voice
  To our ears re-echoing creeps;
From the first soft song to the last sweet speech
  That died upon thy lips.

" Though absent in body, our spirits are one,
  And still at our Father's throne
We bow in prayer and thou in praise;
  Sweet child, we yet are one."

www.ingramcontent.com/pod-product-compliance
Lightning Source LLC
Chambersburg PA
CBHW021044030726
47496CB00006B/1685